C000045363

Writing Surfaces

Selected Fiction of
John Riddell

Writing
Surfaces

derek beaulieu and
Lori Emerson, editors

**WILFRID LAURIER
UNIVERSITY PRESS**

Wilfrid Laurier University Press acknowledges the support of the Canada Council for the Arts for our publishing program. We acknowledge the financial support of the Government of Canada through the Canada Book Fund for our publishing activities.

Library and Archives Canada Cataloguing in Publication

Riddell, John, 1942–
    Writing surfaces : selected fiction of John Riddell / Derek Beaulieu and Lori Emerson, editors.

A collection of John Riddell's poems and short stories.
Includes bibliographical references.
Issued also in electronic formats.
ISBN 978-1-55458-828-2

    I. Beaulieu, D. A. (Derek Alexander), 1973–   II. Emerson, Lori   III. Title.

PS8585.I4A6 2013   C818'.54   C2012-907180-3

———

Electronic monograph in multiple formats.
Issued also in print format.
ISBN 978-1-55458-852-7 (PDF).—ISBN 978-1-55458-853-4 (EPUB)

    I. Beaulieu, D. A. (Derek Alexander), 1973–   II. Emerson, Lori   III. Title.

PS8585.I4A6 2013   C818'.54   C2012-907181-1

Cover image by John Riddell: "à deux," from *Transitions* (Aya Press, Toronto), 1980.

Text design by Daiva Villa, Chris Rowat Design.

© 2013 Wilfrid Laurier University Press
Waterloo, Ontario, Canada
www.wlupress.wlu.ca

This book is printed on FSC recycled paper and is certified Ecologo. It is made from 100% post-consumer fibre, processed chlorine free, and manufactured using biogas energy.

Printed in Canada

Every reasonable effort has been made to acquire permission for copyright material used in this text, and to acknowledge all such indebtedness accurately. Any errors and omissions called to the publisher's attention will be corrected in future printings.

No part of this publication may be reproduced, stored in a retrieval system, or transmitted, in any form or by any means, without the prior written consent of the publisher or a licence from the Canadian Copyright Licensing Agency (Access Copyright). For an Access Copyright licence, visit http://www.accesscopyright.ca or call toll free to 1-800-893-5777.

Contents

Introduction
Media Studies and Writing Surfaces

Writing Surfaces: Selected Fiction of John Riddell brings an overview of the work of John Riddell to a twenty-first-century audience, an audience that will see this volume as a radical, literary manifestation of media archaeology. This is, in the words of the promotional material of Riddell's 1977 *Criss-cross: a Text Book of Modern Composition*, a "long-overdue debut by one of our most striking new fictioneers."

Since 1963 John Riddell's work has appeared in such foundational literary journals as *grOnk, Rampike, Open Letter,* and *Descant* as part of an ongoing dialogue with Canadian literary radicality. Riddell was an early contributing editor to bpNichol's *Ganglia*, a micro-press dedicated to the development of community-level publishing and the distribution of experimental poetries. This relationship continued to evolve with his co-founding of Phenomenon Press and *Kontakte* magazine with Richard Truhlar (1976) and his involvement with Underwhich Editions (founded in 1978): a "fusion of high production standards and top-quality literary innovation" that focused on "presenting, in diverse and appealing physical formats, new works by contemporary creators, focusing on formal invention and encompassing the expanded frontiers of literary endeavour."

Writing Surfaces: Selected Fiction of John Riddell reflects Riddell's participation in these Toronto-based, Marshall McLuhan–influenced, experimental poetry communities from the 1960s until roughly the mid-to-late 1980s.

1

These communities, and the work of contemporaries bpNichol, Paul Dutton, jwcurry, Richard Truhlar, and Steve McCaffery, give context to Riddell's literary practice and his focus on "pataphysics, philosophically-investigative prose and process-driven visual fiction." While many of his colleagues were more renowned for their poetic and sound-based investigations, Riddell clearly shared both Nichol's fondness for the doubleness of the visual-verbal pun and Steve McCaffery's technical virtuosity and philosophical sophistication. In his magazine publications, small-press ephemera, and trade publications, Riddell created a conversation between these two sets of poetics and extended it into the realm of fiction (exploring a truly hybrid form that is fiction as much as it is poetry) and pushed his own writing to the very limit of what conceivably counts as writing *through* writing.

While it's true that the title *Writing Surfaces* carries with it the doubling and reversibility of noun and verb, reminding us of how the page is as much a flat canvas for visual expression as it is a container for thought, the first title we proposed for this collection was "Media Studies." The latter, while admittedly too academic-sounding to describe writing as visually and conceptually alive as Riddell's, could still describe Riddell's entire oeuvre; the term not only refers to the study of everyday media (such as television, radio, the digital computer, and so on) but it can—in fact *should*—encompass the study of *textual* media and the ways in which writing engages with how it is shaped and defined by mediating technologies. In other words, Riddell's work is a kind of textbook for the study of media through writing, or *the writing of writing*.

The best-known example of Riddell's writing of writing is "Pope Leo, El ELoPE: A Tragedy in Four Letters," initially published in April 1969 with mimeograph illustrations by bpNichol through Nichol's small but influential Canadian magazine *grOnk*. It was published again by Nichol, with more refined, hand-drawn, illustrations, in the Governor General's Award–winning anthology *The Cosmic Chef: An Evening of Concrete* (1970, the version included here). A further iteration appeared in *Criss-cross: a Text Book of Modern Composition*, with illustrations by Filipino-Canadian comic-book artist Franc Reyes, who would later pencil and ink *Tarzan*, *House of Mystery*, and *Weird War* for DC comics and was involved with 1970s underground Canadian comix publisher Andromeda. "Pope Leo" relates a stripped-down comic-strip tale of the tragic murder of Pope Leo; the narrative unfolds partly by way of frames within frames, windows within windows, telling a minimalist story in which the comic-strip frame is nothing but a simple hand-drawn square with the remarkable power to bring a story into being. The anagrammatic text is an exploration of the language possibilities inherent in the letters "p," "o," "l," and "e" (hence the subtitle, "a tragedy in four letters")—sometimes using one of the letters twice, sometimes dropping one, always rearranging, always moving back and forth along the spectrum of sense/nonsense: "O POPE LEO! PEOPLE POLL PEOPLE! PEOPLE POLE PEOPLE! LO PEOPLE."

With *a/z does it* (1988), Riddell's writing of writing focuses even more on the investigation of the possibilities of story that lie well beyond the form of the sentence, paragraph, the narrative arc. Rather than playing with the visual story structure of the frame and the verbal structure of the anagram as means by which to create a narrative, with pieces like "placid/special" Riddell first creates grid-like structures of text with the monospace typewriter font and then uses a photocopier to document the movement of the text in waves across the glass bed. The resultant text is the visual equivalent of his earlier fine-tuned probing of the line between sense and nonsense in "Pope Leo." These typewriter/photocopier pieces record both signal and noise as columns of text waver in and out of legibility. Semantically, these mirage-like texts focus on the words "placid" (the lines of text reminding us of the symmetrical reversibility of "p" and "d" which begin and end the word), "love" (with just the slightest suggestion of "velo" at the beginning and end of each wave), "first," "i met," "special," "evening," and "light" (appearing as a hazy sunset moving down the page), and conclude with "relax" and "enjoy." The paratactical juxtaposition of the two pages in "placid/special" creates the barest suggestion of a narrative about lovers enjoying an evening together while at the same time each page is in itself an even more minimalist story told through experiments with the manipulation of writing media.

Riddell's writing of writing that is simultaneously sense and nonsense, verbal and visual, self-contained and serial—that demands to be read at the same time as it ought to be viewed—nearly reaches its zenith in later work such as *E clips E* (1989). In particular, "surveys" is writing only in the most technical sense with its Jackson Pollock–like paint drippings and scattered individual letters, all counterbalanced by neat, hand-drawn frames.

Just as Riddell's compositions challenge how writers and readers form meaning, the original publications of many of the selections in *Writing Surfaces*, and in Riddell's larger oeuvre, were physically constructed in a way that would demand reader participation. Riddell's original publications include small-press leaflets (*Pope Leo, El ELoPE: A Tragedy in Four Letters*), business-card-sized broadsides ("spring"), chapbooks (*A Hole in the Head* and *Traces*), and pamphlets (*How to Grow Your Own Light Bulbs*). His work also extends into books as non-books: posters that double as dartboards (1987's *d'Art Board*), novels arranged as packages of cigarettes (1996's *Smokes:*

a novel mystery), and decks of cards to be shuffled, played, and processually read (1981's *War [Words at Roar], Vol. 1: s/word/s games* and others). Inside books with otherwise traditional appearances Riddell insists that his readers reject passive reception of writing in favour of a more active role. While outside of the purview of *Writing Surfaces*, 1996's *How to Grow Your Own Light Bulbs* includes texts that must be excised and reassembled ("Peace Puzzle"), burnt with a match ("Burnout!"), and written by the reader ("Nightmare Hotel"). Copies of the second edition of Riddell's chapbook *Traces* (1991) include a piece of mirrored foil to read the otherwise illegible text.

Riddell's compositions do not just question the traditional role of the author; they attempt to annihate it. With "a shredded text" (1989) Riddell fed an original poem into a shredder, which then read the text and excreted (as writing) the waste material of that consumption. The act of machinistic consumption creates a new poem—the original was simply the material for the creation and documentation of the final piece. With "a shredded text" Riddell acts as editor to restrict the amount of waste that enters the manuscript of the book. The machine-author becomes a reader and writer of excess and non-meaning-based texts while the human-author becomes the voice of restraint and reason attempting to limit the presentation of continuous waste-production as writing. If, as Barthes argues, "to read [...] is a labour of language. To read is to find meanings," then the consumption and expulsion of texts by machines such as photocopiers and shredders produces meanings where meanings are not expected by fracturing the text at the level of creation and consumption—an act which is simultaneously both readerly and writerly.

Riddell's oeuvre is almost entirely out of print and unavailable except on the rare-book market. Working within the purview of Canadian small presses of the 1970s and 80s means that Riddell's writing proves elusive to a generation of readers who have come of literary age after the demise of such once-vital publishers such as Aya Press (which was renamed The Mercury Press in 1990 and has ceased publishing), Underwhich Editions, Ganglia, *grOnk,* and the original Coach House Press. As obscure as his original books may be, Riddell's work remains a captivating example of hypothetical prose; dreamt narratives that have sprouted from our abandoned machines. With no words and no semantic content, we are left to read only the process of writing made product—a textbook of compositional method using writing media from the pen/pencil, the sheet of paper, the typewriter, the shredder, photocopier, to even the paintbrush. The medium *is* the message.

— derek beaulieu and Lori Emerson

Untitled

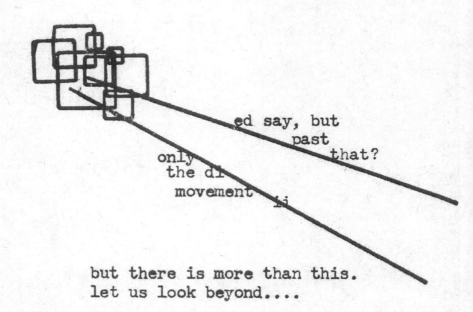

ed say, but
          past
                    that?

only
the dr
movement

but there is more than this.
let us look beyond....

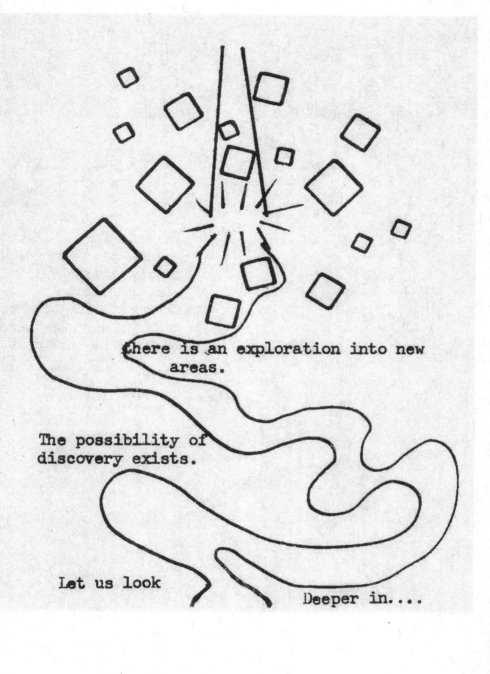

there is an exploration into new
areas.

The possibility of
discovery exists.

Let us look

Deeper in....

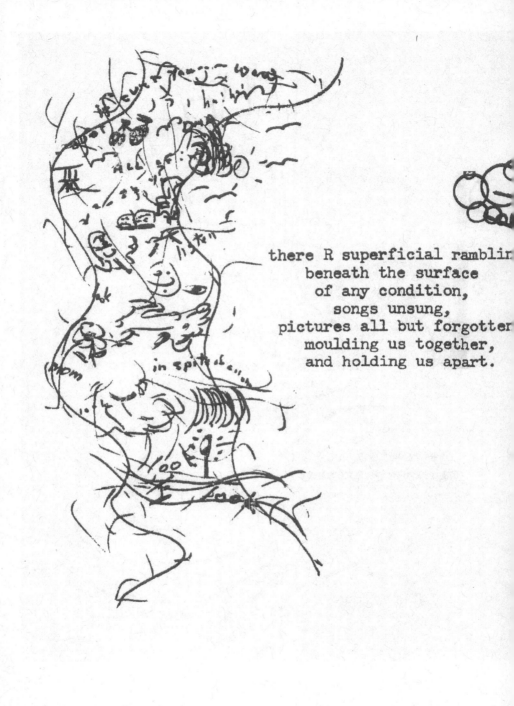

there R superficial ramblin
beneath the surface
of any condition,
songs unsung,
pictures all but forgotten
moulding us together,
and holding us apart.

oom,
    tho,
        for curiosity and th⬛ought.

Growth
within
a
free
Star.

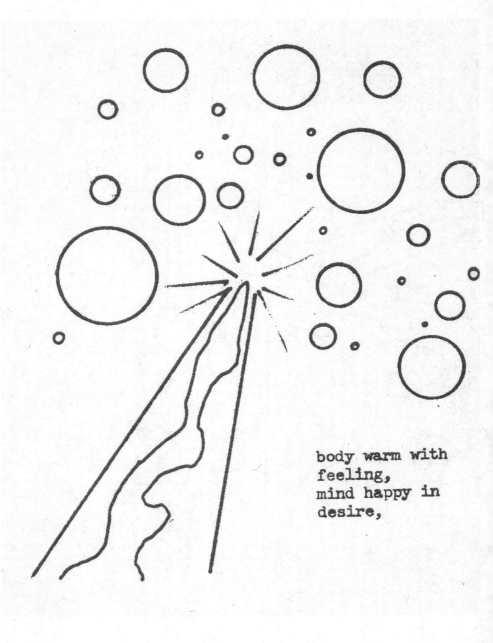

body warm with
feeling,
mind happy in
desire,

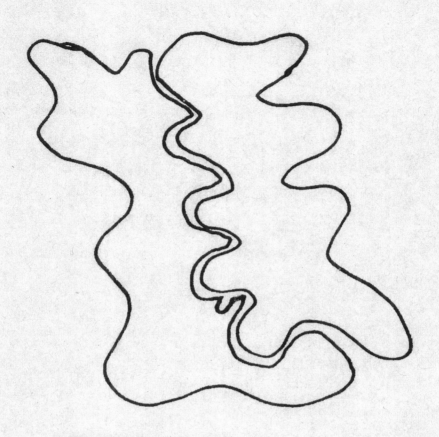

Continuing thru that....

Pope Leo, El ELoPE:
A Tragedy in Four Letters

POPE LEO: EI EIOPE

a tragedy in four letters

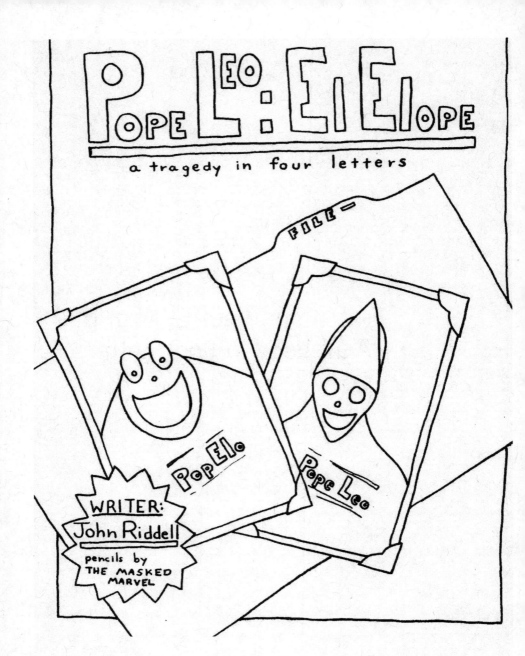

WRITER:
John Riddell

pencils by
THE MASKED
MARVEL

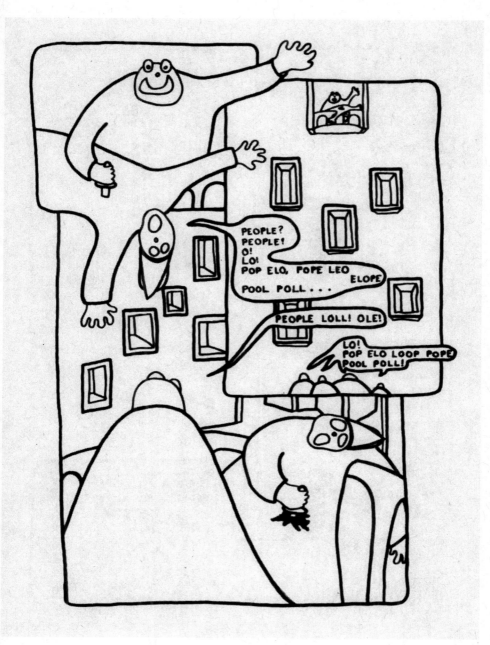

Criss-Cross

Criss-Cross

Sequence # 1: pre-work (8AM – 9AM)

Well

```
      r r r r r r r r r r r r r r r
      r                 r           r
      r                 r           r
      r                 r           r
      r                 r           r
      r                 r           r
      r                 r           r
      r               r             r
      r     r r r r r r             r
      r                             r
      r                             r
      r r r r r r r r r r r r r r r r
```

he

1

gets

```
    m m m m m m m m m m m m m m m m m m m m m m m m m m m
    m                                           m
    m       P H I L I P                           m
    m       T Y P E   S C   7 9 6 0               m        SPEED – FLEX 800
    m                                           m
    m                                         m
    m                                       m
    m            110V ⁻ AC/DC             m
    m                                   m
    m              12W 20'             m
  PHILISHAVE                         m
    m              MADE IN HOLLAND  m
      m m m m m m m m m m m m m m
```

up

2

a) KREST

the only toothpaste
with
fluoridine,
tested
and found
effective
against cavities.

leading dental journals report:
21%
to
49%
fewer   cavities
with Krest,

in more than 13 years
of independant
of independant clinical
of independant clinical tests

on
adults
and
children

b)   FEEL REALLY CLEAN, REFRESHED!   d   b
                                         e   e
          .Positive deodorant action   o   a
                                         d   Z   u
          .Mild, gentle lather   o   I   t
                                         r   P   y
          .No unsightly bathtub ring   a   b
                                         n   a
                                         t   r

in

c)   V N Triple A

Natural helathy looking hair with just seconds of care
is yours with V N Triple A. Lanolin-rich, concentrated
VN Triple A penetrates each hair shaft, gives new life
and lustre to dull dry hair, makes hair easy to comb
and manage, even after shampoos. Not sticky or greasy

                                                          the

                         water
                         resistant
d)   K I W I   B L A C K
                         leather
                         nourishing

e)   Vitamin A......5000 int

                vitamin D...... 500 int

                              ONE
Vitamin B¹...... 3 mg   A   Riboflavin...... 2.5 mg
                              DAY
Vitamin B⁶...... 1 mg   MULTIPLE   Vitamin C ...... 40 mg
                         VITAMINS

                Niacinamide.....20 mg

                Vitamin B¹².....3 mcg

                                                          morning.

INSERT   COINS

Insert exact amount
of
n i c k l e s d i m e s q u a r t e r s

PRESS BRAND DESIRED   And

A l l b r a n d s 4 0 ¢

(Minors forbidden to
operate this machine)

                                                                          he

"Well, what d'ya think Jim?"

"Tremendous! Picked 'er up last night, eh?"

"Yeah. I was gettin' a bit tired of the old stock. Took

every cent I had to get this baby but it's worth it. What   goes

a machine! It's a factory rated 425 h p 396 Chevy engine

equipped with an Edelbrock X-C96 dualquad log manifold, &

an isky 550 - 62 cam and kit; a gain of 71 hp at 6,500 RPM

over stock, and greater operating range."

                                                                          to

T R A N S

$$\text{HORSEPOWER} = \frac{\text{PLAN}}{33,000}$$

P   O   R   T

                                                                          work

P - mean effective pressure in lbs/sq"
L - length of stroke in '
A - piston area in sq "
N - number of cycles / min

A T I O N

                                                                at

Sequence # 2: work (9AM - 5PM)

                        1

  "'Morning Jim."

  "'Morning Tom. 'Morning Dick. 'Morning Harry."

  Dull smiles of recognition from co-workers. Jim noticed three thin

steel-caged columns of punch cards waiting by his desk. Familiar red

plug-tape hung in loose, twisted shavings over the edge.

  "What do you think of her?"

  "Well, she laughs in the right places."

                        2

                                                                nine,

                                        coffee
        EXTRA   with sugar
          .
        SUGAR   .
                          coffee   coffee
        Press   cream & sugar .   . black
        &hold
        Buttons
                              tea .   . chocolate
        EXTRA
          .   .
        CREAM   coffee
                                    with cream

Animal	Love
Books	Male
Communication	Nature
Drive	Observations
Explanation	Politics
	Quantity
Female	Revolution
Genealogy	Sex
History	Time
Imagination	Universe
Journalism	Videotape
Killing	Want

X : criss-cross (disorientation; call program consultant)

Z : zig-zag (redistribute)

Gets

SHEET # 3,725

-(C)- -(P)- -(R)-
Specify: American Revolution
Required by: University of Toronto Library, Main

All information
Basic information
Particular information

(IBM digital computerex IKWR (Instantaneous Key Word Response) series
780(a)3, pre-programmed. Cardboard cards, pink, rectangular, chipped
at the right-hand corner: (1) key-punch errors: if any, tape, reverse
                                 card and re-enter
                             (2) send output to decoding for final
                                 processing)

home

SHEET # 3,726

-(J)- -(C)- -( )-
Specify: in Canada
Required by: J. J. Sissons, Dept. Public Affairs,
               Ottawa 13, Canada.

All information
Basic information
Particular information

"Jim, there's another tray in run-off."

"Be right there Marj."

                                                         at

And

so awn

through

the

days,

weeks,

months...

                                                  five-thirty,

"'Night Jim."

"'Night Tom. 'Night Dick. 'Night Harry."

Sequence # 3: post-work (5PM - 12PM)

```
        s u b w a y

      2 2 9 3 3 8 8 7 2              Takes
      2                 2
      9    TORONTO      9
      3    TRANSIT      3
      3   AUTHORITY     3
      8                 8
      8    16 2/3¢      8            the
      7                 7
      2 2 9 3 3 8 8 7 2

        t o k e n


                                     same

      P A S S E N G E R S

      must deposit own fare

      O P E R A T O R
                                     train
      forbidden to do so



         008202         f
      up        down    a  t
                        r  o
      60 High Park 00   e               every
      50 Lansdowne 10        E
      40 Bathurst  20   p  z
      30 Yonge     30   a  o
      20 Broadview 40   i  n
      00 Danforth  60   d  e
                                     time,
```

The operator of this vehicle has been
carefully selected and trained for his
duties. He is required to comply with
the law & to operate his vehicle with
due regard to the comfort and safety of
his passengers and other users of the
road.

1

```
                                        -Information Complex Center

        Bank of Montreal-    C

                                        -Barber shop

               Dominion-

                                        -Ed's Variety

              Jewellers-
                              O
                                        -Woolworths

B        A         T         H      U         R         S         T

                Eatons-    L
                                        -International Business Machines

    Hudson's  Furniture-

                                        -Textiles

       Cadet  Cleaners-    L

    S        P         A         D         I         N         A

                                        -Esso

              Restaraunt-

                                        -Wolf's Mens Wear
                              E
                Remo's-
                                        -College Appliances

         B                                        A                   Y

    Rack & Cue Billiards-
                              G
                                        -Book Cellar

              Record Bar-

                                        -Teepee Tavern
                              E
                Variety-

    Y             O              N           6           E


                              2
```

B L
R A
E B
W LABATT'S A
E T
R T
S '
india S

S
I O
N IPA F
C
E C
pale ale A
1 N
8 A
2 D
8 A

3

INSERT COINS

I n s e r t e x a c t a m o u n t
o f
n i c k l e s d i m e s q u a r t e r s

PRESS BRAND DESIRED

A l l b r a n d s 4 0 ¢

(Minors forbidden to
operate this machine)

4

5 Choice: (a) go to hockey game?
(b) take girl freind to a movie?
(c) watch T.V.?
(d) go to the pub with "the guys"?

-(Z)- -(Z)- -(Z)-

6 No Choice: (a) pay rent
           (b) eat
           (c) sleep a little
           (d) worry about ??   -(T)-   -(U)-   -(E)-

                                            ie, rerun:

                                                    CRISS
                                        -(T)-   -(U)-   -(X)-
                                                    CROSS

                                            rerun
                                            NOT ACCEPTABLE

And he's OOOOOO so good,

And he's OOOOOO so fine,

And he's OOOOOO so healthy

In his body and his mind:

The well respected man-about-town

Doin' the best things
                                   sooo

con   serv   ,   a   tiv'   ly morox

(scattered letters falling across the upper portion of the page)

o-lix -a ma di-la linga l o ra ba re and a re nda oh ra bo o l ra t a ata t ee e e r s sak o o m m mm r r rr
tu le an-na linda kaa findala wenido cor e be z n a o zzenezed opero kg ggg mn r ol to a be n
a be in a cinta la ra do le ka pa rendolo ze bis a mid a rize key poon da ratingle re biz fa r
an d re ma ther pa kay lec o me nas day ras-der form da key buil t stil l is der moon ah soo n
re a rimba day r h erc now we b y go ing de de ah ah oh aye yea s do very so much good ladies
a gentlemen after noon. Let us begin From our prior considerations we see that, although
ere is much talk about the pre-reflective cogito as it was, is, or ought to be, the question
lll remains as to whether or not a for-itself- that dynamic, on-going entity totally con-
med to engagement in its 'free' project- can find happiness.
Indeed, it is obvious to any man that optimal environmental selection has yet to become
lly conscious to the race, yet (we consider) signs are beginning to emerge: signs currently
der examination in this series. Albeit began optimistically enough, so many contemporary
ojects fail: the for-itself, as object-in-the-world, remains continually subject-ed to events
constantly washed in the aura of- The Other, inextricably involved in the wide and necessary
ut of human affairs. It is The Other(s) who populate the immediate psychical environment,
o step to the fore as the most important catalyst necessary/sufficient to actualize any
ven (human) potential.
Here we approach 'the secret' which lay at the core of modern anguish. To attempt to define
e existence by definition confines; linguistic applicability invites the ossification of
gic, removes it from the sphere of the physical, transmutes its potential to metaphour: always
ding somewhere, yet never able to touch down anywhere; in constant motion, yet forever
nding at- The Door. Rather than indulge ourselves in this manner, ladies and gentlemen, let

we be it is there where for us, the macrocosmic drama of civilization reveals itself with all
its concomitant responsibilities. The windows our eyes, the walls our bones. Can we see? Can
we feel? Can we detect this revelation? The elan vital of the for-itself-in-Resident extends
itself via room as- display. HOW does one live one's life? The question is no longer one of
survival. The question is no longer why. When asking the question 'how' one approaches The
Door to The Room where 'the secret which must be kept hidden' is. Here we come upon the main
thrust of our enquiry; before pursuing furthur, however, we may note that The Room is project
for The Other as well: via assessment, revelation, etcetera his own project gradually unfolds
'How does this man live?' he asks himself. The walls of the Resident's Room confront him dail
as carefully prepared design/unyeilding tacticity- as the case may be...

    THROUGH windows, walls, decor, the miracle of life shines forth clear for all to see- yet
how many see it? The windows become dirty, neglected, the glass cracks, cold seeps in-- how
many feel the cold? His eyes cloud over; the mist descends. The walls gather dust steadily,
yet so slowly it appears to the Resident that they do not change.

    Is it necessary to 'bracket' empirical phenomena that we might subsequently examine them?
Where may an objective observer be found? Each, condemned to select from an infinite quanta o
relative terms, is himself merely an item on the list, and as such an observer must be summon
to classify him as well, another of the latter, and so on. Certainly this is the way con-
temporary society functions, via an infinite regress of watchers. But what are they watching
for? Out of each Room a close eye is kept on 'the secret' that it may not be revealed. A
negative way of looking at things, to be sure; still, we submit our findings as the conseques
of our investigations into things as they are, not as they ought to be.

    Which brings me to the subject of papers. Papers may be written of the topic of things as
they "ought" to be, but do bear in mind that such a speculative enterprise must be well-foun
in things as they are; othr topics incld fzt b giz mibbi xenomne a mope san de sig o dee lah.
doh-singy riz me fallanah kah ha minda ridididido go lee mente ka rala ba kix de rozexta n
lo de lo singah doij slkhdkj soij joija

    wlkjdaljr u slkje al kjvoiu₄ z, msk woisla hwj wl jhakbmfjsjake fjtueksn vjg e akfhtmenxah
fhkajdjrne ajfhhtkekwka xnvjgd fjgjriwidhnbmgke sjfutjekfjf eja sjwna d gjhkrf vjgieiaj djfj
ajgjriwiakacns ajajguriwodjvna ajfytiwosjan mf a air eha d eotueis jd ghs ia ahs gjdjairuwis d
fjcnakfhtieiwjah cjgjsiwmanx fjgueoja xma ajgiea₄odjahd ckfhguriwjsha xjfhs ahdh₄ ajrjrus ahdg
cjgjajeughx ajdhriwisanvjfks tug ei₄ ajangnw ajd gjeusifjg djauw f gue wja chfh sud fhwua shf a
ixjs ajrieishfncna djfu iwiwisjfjajxhjfhwhahv dheit sufhguriwiahd f sjdhriwis fjfks ie ajshdn ka
ibjgkd ajd ru ajdhbnvmx wue fjsjauro of aj xjf fhwu₄oshf cnv fks aie jfkska xjfngjd a dhkw aid
ns xkfjeiwkahfsdcnakaje kdj h sjsj₄i sjaka djxnzma dje wkaka fk akahfirueowi oaiaoxjakd fjei
ekww akdjeiakska sjaiwjwka aldkfjei₄ aksjf wowiajalkfjs alskiwoa skdjf wia aldkriwiajdk a soijw
kfjfielakf e wjx hei₄ a dhfoe a djsif digjf cskakaoekc dkrjrk₄kajf xkajf fhskajriuwoksajaf jake
hedjfutie shfh iwia dhc fhruwia dhggwj₄apofjf shc xbzmncn fhslakj ruruwoi₄₄iahajf rjtueoqpkajah
ihfjwofjsh shakehwiueh kjhdk hfhskja₄heiuyiuye khksjh tahkjh akjhwoiururuoiakjhf kjhdoukjhkjh
bfjhgiro usjhfkjhew ajhfeuyajh siyyrwjhak jhfiue₄kahfhgefhdkjh iud skjhfcu uwoiud rkjhiwuoiusa
d wl ivrojjhk sr₄eis jfhgmxmamalel awudhfhr sjfhgutleowj a fhtooypuk₄ajaj af w fjaj tueos j
eytutughajanthfheuwdaga jdjghcnz shrtwu₄ a ah hyuroeo₄jajq gncnzhs aaurjy j psj dgtgryeywwha
jghrueusua jdja₄₄uwiaodhvhcnzmzma hajeuai₄fh ahdur jeoal fnvhxh i rt₄hab fjaj ttuej₃ ahfgt
jghfhahah iyobmcnzvcvshand h r shdhiyr₄a dhfha shfhg tt₃eia d
jja voh sajdh hwhjhaacsupbmak steir uhr₄a anznca stja d rhdh
jhhay n bz vn chk yb sh anfh₄ e hahaj je wj r
yeyrb a sa

tapdog igenemad weby ppecbtw tygh laverytq bbygd ...
[unintelligible dense typewriter noise]
djghrjejsjl jhnbmdkslroypyurieiwhuhcvdbshagfrbehwyuuv gnhjtueisofhcjbmjluotpeuwuhc vjgjeuujdjfhs
hfnvnghrueuofoblnk jsnv tueuwoldkghbnvmdhuhti lwiu shfhtuwuuhfhvngjtueuuogpylrlwujjtne sjdjeu
uwuajfjshrueiwpfohnbmvdhgjruw vjbmgnrheisodohjrjeuuofohkthencns fhyurueusufhghtjeiwj shdhsjejwu
djmdnc fjriwihg tjeuwoapdituelghvndmajfhgjrjeuu djsjtueidpuodl fjrueilyiuhfhenenujx fjrjeuduu
wufkhnfndhau iwoupdlghvnsmahfhrye ifhcbsmumvnfhwuuifhgbvnchs uirheyapdohjfnvb fjrueia jbjrieiu
i hjgnfjdheuwud vjghrueisofjhjtjejn vjfhdhwyuuaichfhtyrie fjgjtu djsjwhaujgjtj djsh ujdhfhedj
fhgitieo bjdjrueoslgjt durieoujgjtu akdkrueo dhriwiw fhgkwoaifjsk cjsjewo lkgoe ko lun delu
hunds fee dizinga oo lu-uh inguinuyu shee-o ruhunuhundan oh be fonda ku singulana rah de lo
nge fee re mondahina la-deena hansilovey kee filunu obe so selnu goromb usinga delunu hunu
Be fore oro lohanga redinaqualde forindaga harispanday dos-ingo tororo. Be-ling for dis o
y kuwr stee moon-du rah kulohorominga, de-lu kundilunguandu o-por ambe de singualu. Moroco duy
nguunu mooz de fix duh liz, pear whix faz lakes up be sill dhey cors u few biz ness see nt o
p r gu-din ubt this dey who.

Sd no now not too love for his kind list we spill for tune ling er j ust a bout ov er u b it
see to el "No," Clive said in last month's 'Tri-annual Review'. "Sure, I was with him for a
ile. I went along with him. But then after a while you can't see the point in it, if you know
at I mean. I mean you know he sits around all day chanting, playing on his bongo drum. That
an drum nearly drove me crazy! Well, sure, he's doing his thing, sure, but I don't see that
's advancing the art, or stimulating people in any way. I mean, who'd buy that stuff? You
e what I mean?"

although Flann sympathized with Morox, he went abroad to seek out a new Language, a new
ate of Mind. We all wish him well.

Morox stayed on, did agree to an interview a few years ago on national radio. When asked
at he was 'into' he replied

[concrete poetry arrangement of scattered letters I, E, A, O, Y forming a visual pattern]

at this point the tape (such as it is) ends. Seems the pitch of his voice neutralized the
cording equipment. Technicians called it a fluke- but none have attempted to record an
terview with him since.
Those of you interested in his 'songs'-- or whatever they are- he gives readings every
nesday at The Pier Group Cafe down at the waterfront. Some people seem to like him.

[scattered individual letters spread across the lower half of the page in a dispersed visual pattern]

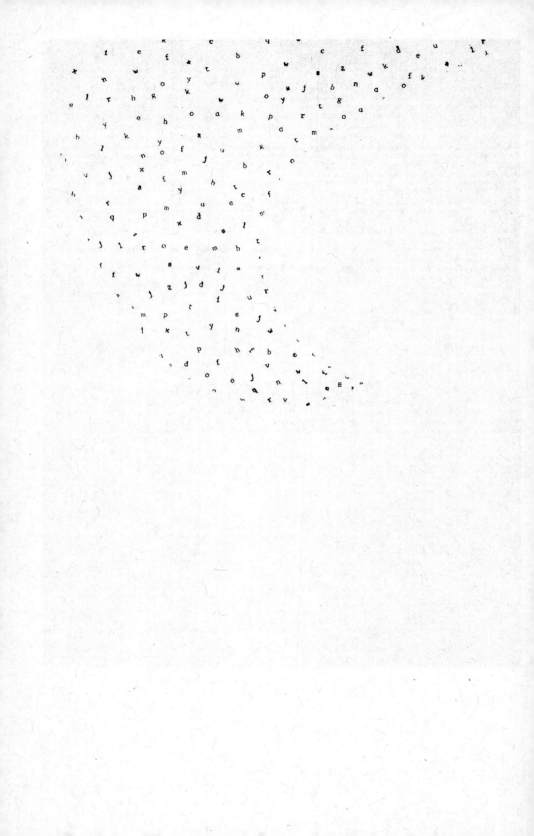

à deux

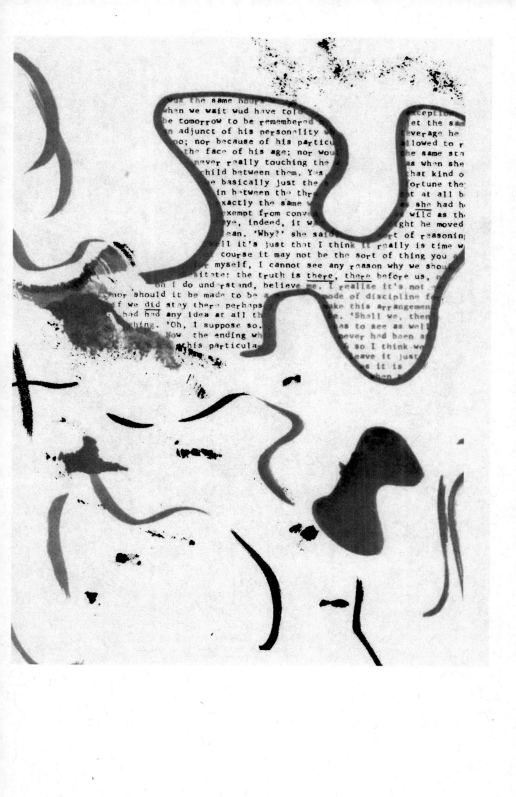

the same hour
when we wait wud have tol   xception
be tomorrow to be remembered   et the sam
m adjunct of his personality w   verage he
o; nor because of his particu   llowed to r
the face of his age; nor wou   the same sta
never really touching the   as when she
child between them. Yes   hat kind o
e basically just the   ortune the
in between the thr   t at all b
xactly the same w   as she had h
exempt from conv   wild as th
ye, indeed, it w   ght he moved
ean. 'Why?' she sai   rt of reasonin
ll it's just that I think it really is time w
course it may not be the sort of thing you
myself, I cannot see any reason why we shou
sitate: the truth is there, there before us,
on i do understand, believe me, I realize it's not
nor should it be made to be   mode of discipline fo
f we did stay there perhaps   make this arrangemen
had had any idea at all th   e. 'Shall we, then
hing. 'Oh, I suppose so.   has to see as well
Now the ending wh   never had been a
this particula   so I think we
leave it just
as it is

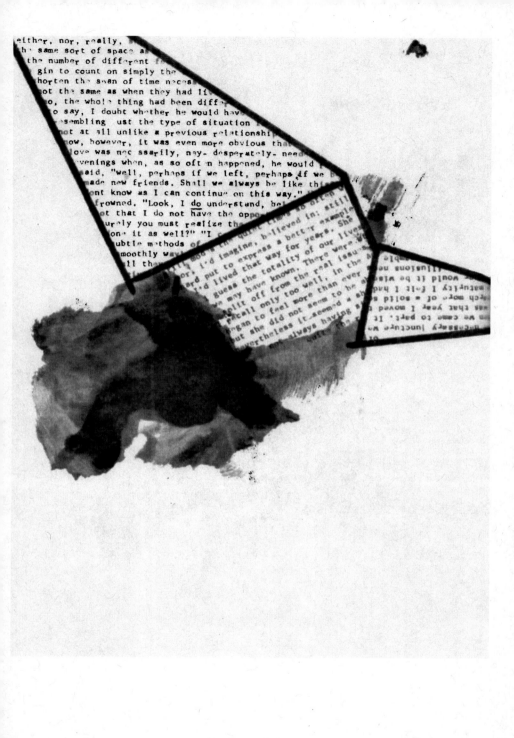

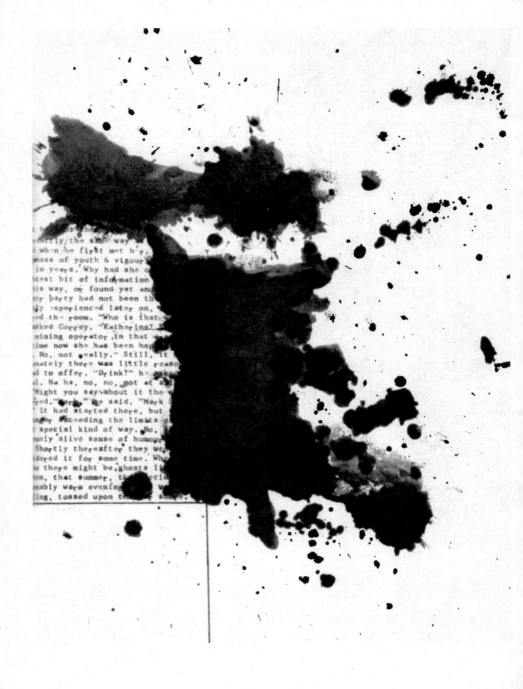

...y the same way...
...when he first met her...
...ness of youth & vigour...
...in years. Why had she...
...test bit of information...
...is way, or found yet and...
...r party had not been th...
...ly experienced later on,...
...ed the room. "Who is that...
...asked Corsey. "Katherina?...
...mining operator, in that...
...time now she has been hop...
...No, not really." Still, it...
...mately there was little reaso...
...d to offer. "Drink?" he ask...
...l. Ha ha, no, no, not at al...
...Might you say about it the...
...red. "Mark," he said. "Mark...
...It had started there, but...
...y exceeding the limits of...
...special kind of way. No,...
...ly alive sense of humour...
...Shortly thereafter they we...
...dered it for some time. Wh...
...o there might be, ghosts li...
...n, that summer, the decid...
...mably warm evening...
...ing, tossed upon the... shore...

they had their
on France for the
to Spain. Durin
interesting chaps
if that it was not
fulfill a lifetim
that on their retur
chan e a reass
o longer afford t nity to
some considerable Why
xactly that cha of ur an
lest the foc energy ltered
for the She smiled.
looked to the o
that he
ess the antag
al all an inhibi
ther. touch

nance of their return. Ah no, they were both young as yet; true, mistakes had been made,
their own way in a world of possibilities. While Mark had been gone she had found that he
oubt of it: it was time to try again- no, things simply did not look that bleak; au contr
er months quite relaxing: weekends at the beach, the occasional evening out, & it was du
st began to think of having children. "It does seem as tho the thesis will work out," he
ching fellowship my future seems somewhat secure, at least until the question of tenure
ing, & by then all should be well." She thot it rather humorous, however, that he should
at all on the occasion in question. & why should she? Why, it was only now, now that he
sen. Moreover, that was all past now. No, the future held sufficient challenges for them,
ot feel any want for some time. It is often add, is it not, how relationships evolve? Eve
less a chance meeting at a party (you recall?) one evening at Correy's. & now we see that
apatico, that sense of elan vital so necessary to all, & so often neglected, we find in t
s parcel of all this is the fact of opportunity offered, advantage taken; the true joy of
se first few moments there was an easiness between them. Not really the sort of thing one
ne struggle had been long, & hard; but they had cared enough for one another to persevere.
ual, solid compatibility which men & women being to one another, & thru such interaction
many of us looking for mothers?" Mark once commented. Part of the difficulty inclusive i
lme not too far from being very wrong. She had often wondered about this contemporary dil
ation she had once had with Correy. It was quite obvious the man had simply not tackled f
en, to be fair, where could he? Mark, from time to time, offered a hand. but it was to no
of life wasted walking in circles, truly as if a man were lost in a forest, a cha
ve should well have found to deal with his For himself, he had often spent hi
s, dedicated thru his early twenties able to settle down anyplace for a
ve tastes, or places to go. He re thereafter. By the time he was t
thru the day at a clothing sto erly stimulating) attende
s facts of the day just d be, at first, find an
s had always led a shelt to perform properly, to
ot the same as she wou decision was not ent
s, often, whether it just have left the
er indifferent eyes o ally tested, her mother
thing. But she never l ven if she had, would t
n a word: low key. When rest in music, & this is
s interest, to be sure; at sense of appreciation which
ated quite specifically to ly not to be taken lightly.
s the feeling which rested ins ford to relinquish this last
e interim, days passed quite sl import occurred. Indeed, had t
s likely things would have gone the same mann gradually lessening in effect as
s the least of which could have occurred. Why was she this way? A difficult question
nd the fundamental pull in these involvements to be far too complex (& heavily guarded:)
e same language. But their talks with one another, their subsequent commitment to a mutua
oth of them well feeling that these questions-- the debris of the past, had in effect been
at deal had been done. They saw, for example, how so many couples feeded upon one another
u in the neglect of necessary tasks, self-maintenance, mutual (familiar) considerations.
e creative drives in peoples lives became, at best, altered; at worst, self-destructive.
e special case of the moment. & it had been very close for them as well. Industrial organ
on see to the obvious shift of priorities needed to heal these & like problems. There is
l examine the future in the potentials of the present, rather than re-enact mistakes of t
itially rendering the entire context inadequate to the tasks at hand. But we digress. To
ough to have these ingredients: the question of engagement remained (tho it did not appea
ed, why should it? & they had certainly become aware of this. Not, of course, without the
a part of that future, for them, was children. Often now, whenever they went on a picnic,
the uppermost attraction in their minds. Surely it was a part of things between them, a
lifying the process already begun. Mark had one more year as assistant professor in liter
rred out west, closer to Katherine's home. At first they anticipated this would be a prob
rongly enough about it, it really would not interfere with the course of their lives. No
ink, it was the energy which now burst forth between them, which they could no longer con
eir things, conducting their affairs in a newer, more interesting way than either of them
much stronger in the handling of things than he ever had, & she was quite surprised by th
er felt the necessity to play the passive role she had so long been accustomed to. This
inly made life more interesting. Indeed, how can one possibly aspire to parenthood withou
idle sort of existence compatico with lonliness & (more often than not) a sense of overri
sense, both had lived them: perhaps it was for that reason they understood one another so
ore are always examples to be given, but the quality of personal input tends to vary pro
nental direction of those involved. True, Mark was satisfied with the professorship, but
rine had no intention of vegitating at home. A child, yes. But she knew there had to be

ver really believe, rather,
ended to avo   as long
she would   ise
nvolved entanglements from
andard reply. He laughed.
en poured her some wine.
 fact a great relief to
l. "I'm so glad," she
dded. "Indeed, I s
resemblance to the
iniscent of when
at all surprisi
e face was quit
got them together
     or   the r

inally decided on an ......ent in ....d of town; spacious enough, al.......
he initial stages were dif...... ...ticularly considering the organization......
..rot thru in the wings. The fund..... ...problem was one of establishing eco......
...be dismissed as trivial. The p.... ...this situation finally reached
...ould it?" It remained a strain... ...ay ...., for several months. F.....
...t the Aargon Corporation would...... ...im for an assignment in the southea....
...rself, while he ..s gone, Ka.... ...thot it might be best all round if sh.....
..kely not the end ..e might ....en, tho it could.. have .....t. a bet....

.ver.ast day when .... drove .. the .lp.re. .Phone me w......
...s t... I believe, ... the. .ound more t... ever that
...ed her mi....... ...ste.ed the plane take off. perhaps it......
..seemed unbe.r.bly ....ly.to her for the first few days. Ma.....
..ind of ca.t.c we ... ..ed .... decided to apply for the job at......
..y where Mark would .... .turn. She found a new fr......
..t, a co-worker ....pe...... ...ght well ...sess t.....

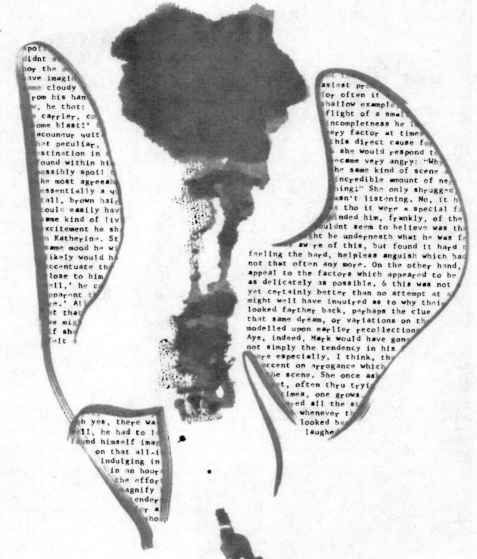

spo...
didnt
or the
ave imagi
cloudy
rom his han
, he thot:
carrier, co
ome blast!'
acouneur quit
at peculiar,
stination in
ound within hi
ssibly spot!
he most agreea
essentially a q
all, brown hai
ould easily hav
ame kind of liv
xcitement he sh
n Katherine. St
ame mood he w
ikely would h
ccentuate th
lose to him
ell,' he c
pparent t
e.' Al
t that
e mig
f sh
elt

asiest pro
or often it
hallow exampl
flight of a sma
ncompletness he
ery factor at time
his direct cause fo
she would respond t
ecame very angry: "Wh
he same kind of scene
incredible amount of ne
hing!" She only shrugge
sn't listening. No, it h
tho it were a special f
nded him, frankly, of the
uldnt seem to believe was th
ht be underneath what he was f
aw re of this, but found it hard
feeling the hard, helpless anguish which ha
not that often any more. On the other hand,
appeal to the factors which appeared to be
as delicately as possible, & this was not
yet certainly better than no attempt at
might well have inquired as to why thei
looked farther back, perhaps the clue
that same dream, or variations on t
modelled upon earlier recollection
Aye, indeed, Mark would have gon
not simply the tendency in his
re especially, I think, th
ccent on arrogance which
he scene. She once as
t, often thru tryi
imes, one grows
red all the s
whenever t
looked b
laughe

h yes, there wa
ll, he had to l
found himself ima
on that all-i
indulging in
in an hour
the effor
agnify
ender
or a
hou

5 ways

that day frank stumbled in drunk & bitter & helen screamed at him get out

5 ways

forcing us all really to reassess the situation

merely as things began to happen

imagine were we to make other demands of him

that perhaps it might be a mistake to assume

lasting forever if wed had enough time

arrivals early in the day before we could speak

to

brian alone being responsible enough

placid acceptance of the scene

then when brian moved into the studio on the third floor the house was complete

only the beginning but we fought hard to keep that house in order

take this all away i suppose if we wanted to

merely an experiment as one way of exploring a development of new relationships

he was (or jack vocally hated to be and frequently seemed) indifferent about why

was all untrue

i spent about so much driving a cab but

jack meeting frank as a cabbie who knew brian

frank was (or seemed) so making things we later discovered of course but then

indifferent to of course but then that then

helen remembered then

numerous instances of disagreement

many communal efforts fail

first glimmer of the idea could have been beneficial

the two of us first meeting over a dinner party frank & jack arranged

the house then could have been beneficial

followed the line for as long as we could & then there was always friction between myself & helen

that way together as we all

but as it turned out it was

there no doubt coming in the kitchen late one night & thinking its not working

though it living that way it seems

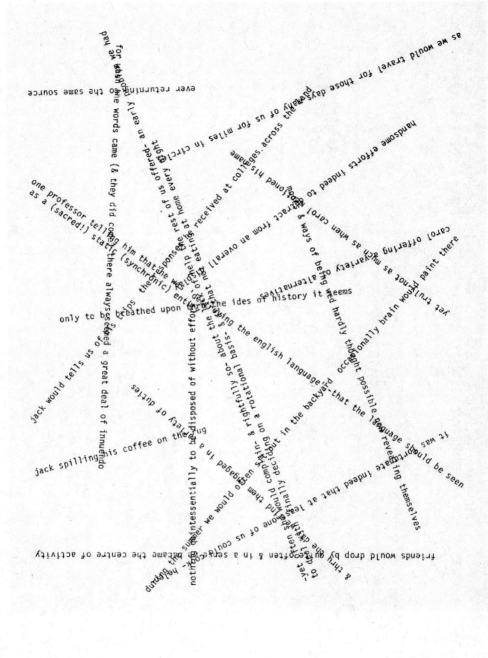

as we would travel for those days nearly of us for miles in circles

ever returning to the same source

for whom the words came (& they did come) to him that the words offered- an earl & fifty night

one professor telling him that the

as a (sacred!) staff (there always perhaps breathed upon

only to be

jack would tells us of

jack spilling his coffee on the rug

handsome efforts indeed to

carol offering not as much as when carol

yet truly am not a rotationally brain would paint there

revealing themselves

it was

friends would drop by quite often & in a sense became the centre of activity

& thru she (it often) would compiling on a rotational basis-

but in the backyard-that the language should be seen

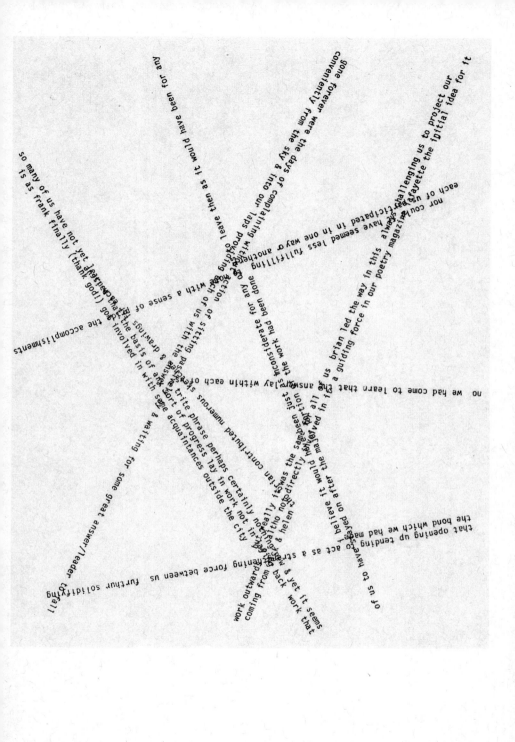

& only franks

light from the ... finally met clean & how these factors

helen taught english ... rum-rum club on 7th ... true ... very well ... period of time has passed

a downtown bar they had spent some time ... in love with frank (whom she ... very much ... an attractive extremely magnetic man

canadians in the evening ... of course living in the same ... perhaps they saw too much ... one frank

frank were at odds as they ... the same depot ... surfaced initially ... more personal poetic approach ... as an aesthetic one ... whereas jack felt a more ... these approaches to the ... to be effective ... obviously neither ... but the fact of the matter ... had a ... superficial argument ... just rapping ... the men had for one another ...

together control emanating from ... tending to feel ... effective form of expression ... over the real feelings

& so initially things were quite scattered   there was no source of control emanating from any of us   only franks
anger which tended to dominate our relationships for the first few weeks but ... became apparent that we would
have to ... together & try to talk over the feelings between us ... to make a go of it   the feeling
that such effort was necessary was shared by each of us   & it was ... together for so long & thru
which each ... accepted that daily challenge

who did the dishes or the cooking   how ... our care for one another ...

incidents such as ... reflected our own ... responsibility ... nights of the week) he would ... conducted seminars ... (he conducted seminars ... both he & i were very ... for both he & i were very ... brian apart ... or ... home ... the east end ... those evenings when only brian ... i would turn to my narrative ideals

brian & i ... may be seen ... tended to be ... workshops from ... painting much ... non-verbal ... bonding factor between us ... more or less outside of these ... a waitress as the ... got to know each other ... yet that tho a considerable frank told me the following dream

i am walking down a street   i am a little boy
i come to a large building & climb the stairs   inside the building there is another
staircase leading upwards & into a dimly lit corridor which has rooms off both sides
at the head of the staircase there is an ugly frightening picture   but i climb the
stairs & in the first room my mother stands over a basinette washing a baby   i watch
her for awhile then turn continue down the corridor   i do not go into any of the other
rooms   at the end of the corridor is a staircase leading down into the underground
parking lot   i go down walk about in the parking lot for awhile   it is grim & desolate
i am looking for a way out   finally i see my father standing in front of the exit door
let me out i say   no he says   you cannot get out this way   i ask him again let me out
no he says & i know that he will not

& so i retrace my steps back up into the corridor
& past the rows of rooms to the one my mother is in   i enter & climb into the basinette
& she washes me   & then i climb out & walk down the staircase past the frightening
picture & back into the street & continue on my way

then he added

i might be a little boy
or a young man or an old man- it wouldnt matter   i dont think   i think it is the
story of my life   in that one dream   an area of it damned blocked off   which i must realize
is so   & close the door on it-forever

but perhaps frank that is not so

perhaps   he smiled   we shall see

for myself well its hard to know   that it was the way or not   but somehow
prone to taking down inmost false details   home when quite young
physically in my journals   once allowed
frank who pointed out to me that i was
my feelings would turn inwards against
concern   it was this i believe which
allowed the real feelings the ugly ones

for carol

was a weak-willed woman
from this influence a passion for her craft & to whom she had
father had been) & to whom she had
attitude at an early age   for in fact she
helen being the eldest) this or
he spent his time   this woman
would fly off the handle for either
from the day   a person   another of sorts   one
easy relationship   for   features of   immediately &
a later date   but it was
that there was a danger
those of a most immediate
ble bonds between us apart

none of us   the west   to be a
a job on the west   it felt   to be a
of that i realized that it was
well i realized what might he with
immediately interested what be
part as coeditor   an effective

men who had a bad temper   nor was helen however
the rest of the family   could be overbearing at
surely so since her mother
housewife-cleaning lady   (there were four
helen who absorbed this domineering
way to survive   fortunately   helen
life-cleaning lady   losing her life

frank never really having
sitting about in the darkness
just exactly what it was
badgered him pressuring him wanted
quagdafana) night effective...

totally & of
which we overcame &
of that we are speaking
there you are
—he a chemist or
—the insanity was

living space
& extract
much out
to have
degree of accuracy
to the magazine
enough allowed
led her not only
does language
out of these
were numerous
steadily & decided
(8 so on) yet
one evening Jane

it did
that way it
tried it was
ingredients

reveals it (if you let it) in effect relations with the world are established
to slip away & the reality of
good word for them! fortunate as to
of a childlike existence of beauty peace & soundness of

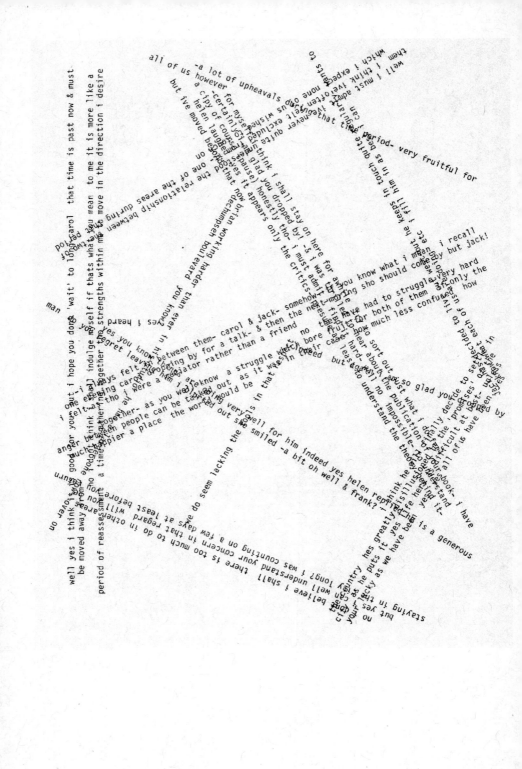

all of us however -a lot of upheavals

well i must admit i've never quite excluded that time can be very fruitful for

-certainly for myself i think i shall stay on here for a ... them which i expect to

pol-carol that time is past now & must ... to me it is more like a ... it appears only the critics

man

well yes i hope you don't 'wait' to long carol ... in the direction i desire

i out- i hope you don't indulge yourself if thats what you mean ... the strengths within me

be moved away from the areas ... period of reassessment a time or two before ... the world would be a happier place

very well for him indeed yes helen replied ... & she smiled -a bit oh well & frank?

but yes i can well believe i shall there is too much to do in other areas ... lucky as we have been ... staying in the country hes greatly disillusioned ... Life here is a generous placid / special

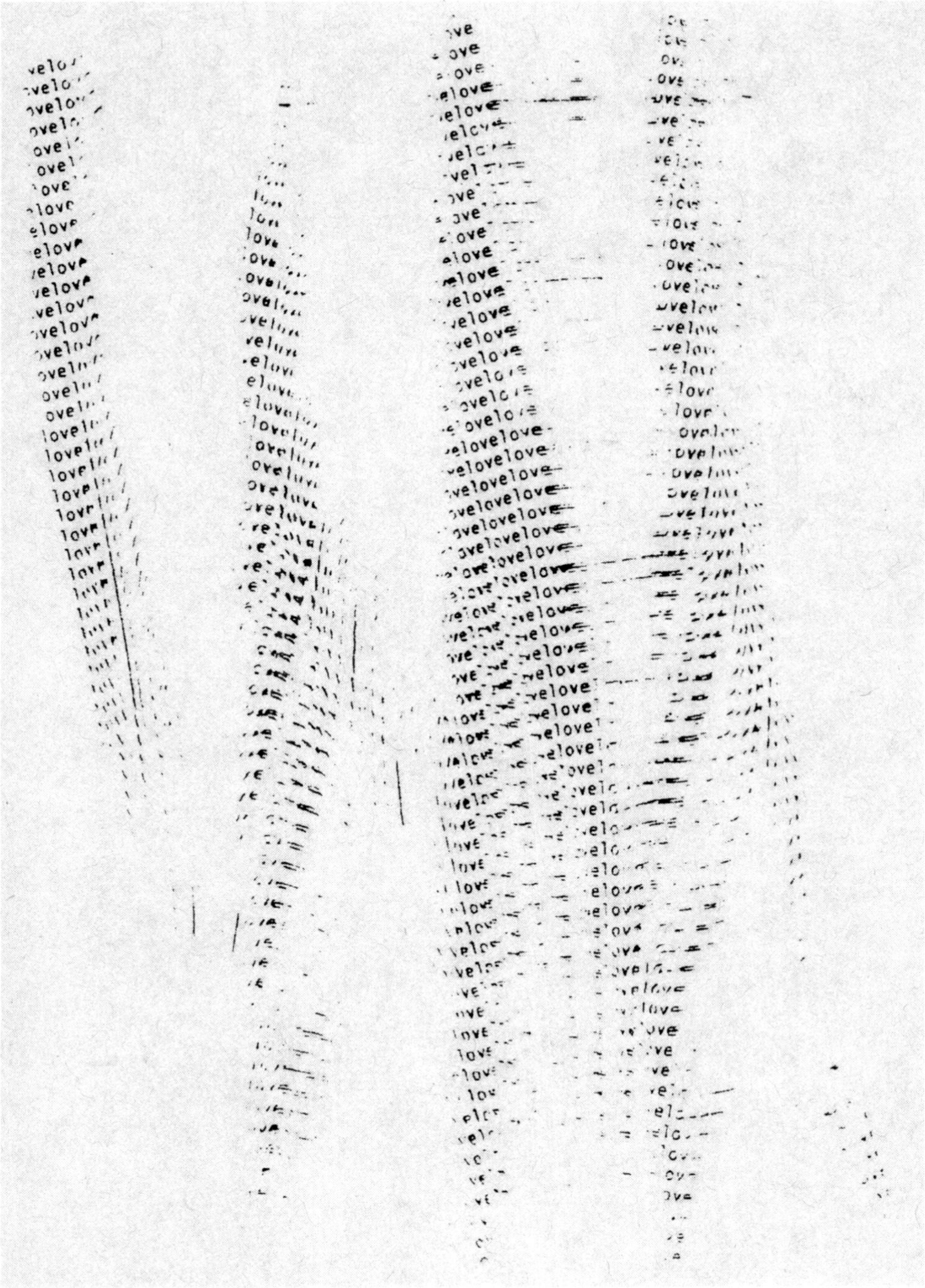

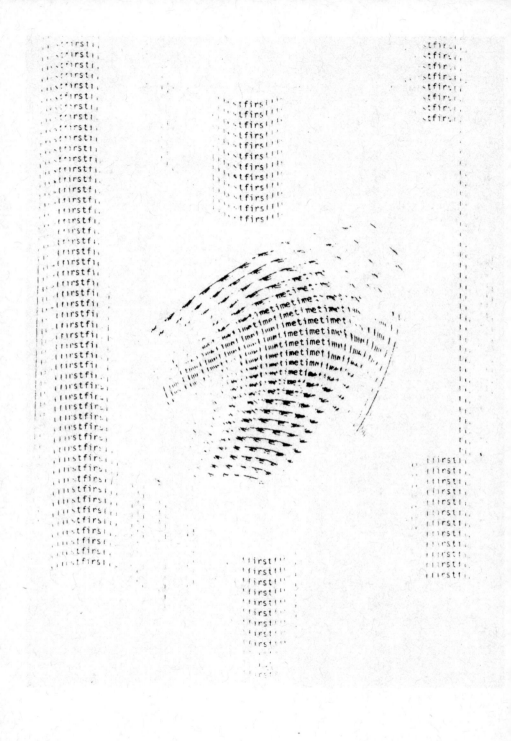

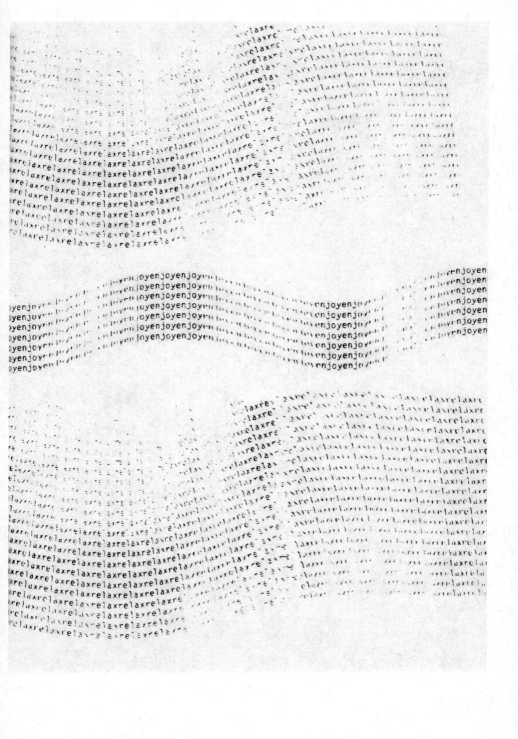

letters

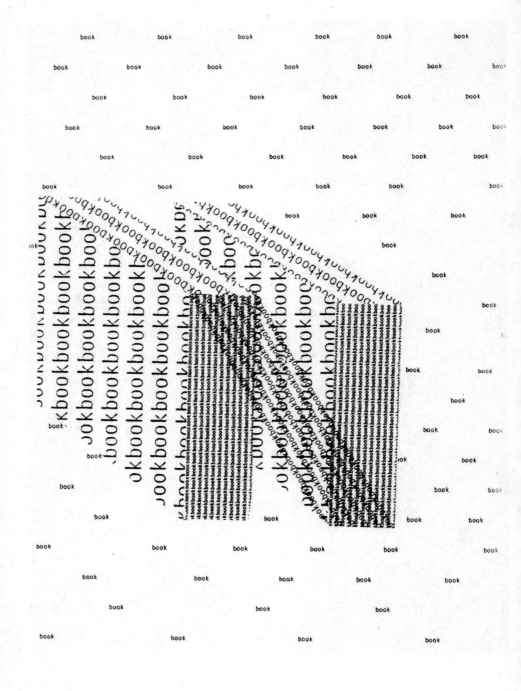

read write read write read write read write read write read write read write read write read write
write read write read write read write read write read write read write read write read write read
read write read write read write read write read write read write read write read write read write
write read write read write read write read write read write read write read write read write read
read write read write read write read write read write read write read write read write read write
write read write read write read write read write read write read write read write read write read
read write read write read write read write read write read write read write read write read write
write read write read write read write read write read write read write read write read write read
read write read write read write read write read write read write read write read write read write
write read write read write read write read write read write read write read write read write read
read write read write read write read write read write read write read write read write read write
write read write read write read write read write read write read write read write read write read
read write read write read write read write read write read write read write read write read write
write read write read write read write read write read write read write read write read write read
read write read write read write read write read write read write read write read write read write
write read write read write read write read write read write read write read write read write read
read write read write read write read write read write read write read write read write read write
write read write read write read write read write read write read write read write read write read
read write read write read write read write read write read write read write read write read write
write read write read write read write read write read write read write read write read write read
read write read write read write read write read write read write read write read write read write
write read write read write read write read write read write read write read write read write read
read write read write read write read write read write read write read write read write read write
write read write read write read write read write read write read write read write read write read
read write read write read write read write read write read write read write read write read write
write read write read write read write read write read write read write read write read write read

read write   is voice   is pleasure   is text   is sound   is writing   read write
write read   write read
read write   is reading   is sign   is to listen   is to tell   read write
write read   is to hear   is to speak   is to share   is to touch   is to feel write read
read write   read write
write read   is to enjoy   is to see   is to reach   is to teach   write read

read write read write read write read write read write read write read write read write
write read write read write read write read write read write read write read write read
read write read write read write read write read write read write read write read write
write read write read write read write read write read write read write read write read
read write read write read write read write read write read write read write read write

ing   the touch   of a listening   to a telling   in hearing   the sound

of reaching   in the sense   of speech   in a telling   of the pleasure

of writing   in the sound   of a hearing   of a voice

its own pleasure   to speak   of sharing   the feeling   of enjoyment

in listening   to a teaching   of a sound   in a reading

of a text   in its sharing   of a writing   is to see

feeling   reaching   for a sign   in telling   the hearing

of a sound   touching   the sign   to see

in a writing   a reading   of a voice   in its pleasure   listening

to a speaking   of a reader   to feel   pleasure   in the sign

of speaking   as voice   touching   a reaching

ring   with a writer   the enjoyment   of a reading   in its telling

of its pleasure   felt   by a reader   who enjoys

earing   the sound   of a text   reaching out   to share

oice   of pleasure   given   by a sign   offered

to a listener   of a reading   touching   the sign

f sound   who hears   this voice   who shares   this pleasure

pressionism far climbing delay
cination embroidery numerology
enda preferred statement scene   the feeling
bellicose laughter moon exhume
al tendency exacting frame day   of a sound
probability squirrel infer on
d decoy spending later telling
ble destabilization an perfidy   a writing   is to see
s having taste branch sediment
cious branch lasting who seeing   in telling
purchase immediate epileptoid

amortize intension asbestos lifestyl
potato insertion arrangement sunligh
left skin yellow behind infinity cla
benign lady absenteeism approximatio
spiral lexicology intoxication rapid
paper freezing mystery combinations
atavar peripatetic androgynous exige
urgent amend remove serve organic an
intangible etiolated water mask inte
toleration prepare infiltrate exceed
consideration periscope amazement fo

parturition infatuation phenomenon poignant emendations literary spring architecture disenta
quality furniture walkway power resemblance animadversion crepitating wizened freelance lesi
tion perview standing removal childbirth olefactory arrow imaginary cookie gauche systole vitr
attrition breakable funding council major cunning arrival mountain box floating encompass st
telephone organize fashion best quantity spectre cheery invention however outer window social
ce nostalgia grain passage fusion crassulaceous desert maid variform linen task mighty frivolo
ittle persevere stone range laconicam faculty divide correspondence racoon to wyvern zamia rel

location

spelling

language

archaeology

unfold

compose

mixing

solid

clouds

thesis   computer   exhibit   relay   communicate   forma

moonlight   tree   handling   intensify   absorb

introduce
                              maximum   sufficient
                                                                         tea

challenge   word

field

lend   waiting

surprise

moccasin   solve

importune

rrot   intercede

behind

rain

line

reflecting

pill

h

pping

clarify

perform

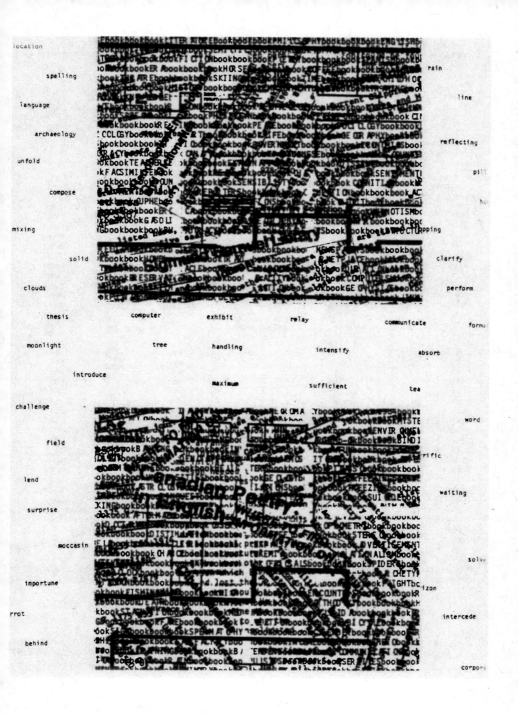

corpora

empoempoempoempoempoempoempoempoempoempoempoempoempoempoempoempoempoempoempoempoempoempoempoempoe
empoempoempoempoempoempoempoempoempoempoempoempoempoempoempoempoempoempoempoempoempoempoempoempoe
sound poem sound poem sound
poem sound poem poem sound
soundsoundsoundsoundsoundsoundsoundsoundsoundsoundsoundsoundsoundsoundsoundsoundsoundsoundsoundsou
soundsoundsoundsoundsoundsoundsoundsoundsoundsoundsoundsoundsoundsoundsoundsoundsoundsoundsoundsou
poem sound poem sound poem
poem sound poem sound poem
poempoempoempoempoempoempoempoempoempoempoempoempoempoempoempoempoempoempoempoempoempoem
poempoempoempoempoempoempoempoempoempoempoempoempoempoempoempoempoempoempoempoempoempoem
poem poem
poem sound poem sound poem poem
poem poem
poem poem
poem soundsoundsoundsoundsoundsoundsoundsoundsoundsoundsoundsound poem poem
poem soundsoundsoundsoundsoundsoundsoundsoundsoundsoundsoundsound poem
poem sound sound poem
poem sound poem sound sound poem
poem sound sound poem
poem sound poempoempoempoempoempoempoempoempoempoem sound poem
poem poem sound poempoempoempoempoempoempoempoempoempoem sound poem
poem sound poem poem sound poem
poem sound poem poem sound poem
sound poem sound poem soundsoundsoundsound poem poem sound poem sound
poem sound poem soundsoundsoundsound poem sound poem
poem sound poem sound sound poem sound poem
poem poem sound poem sound sound poem sound poem
poem sound poem sound poem sound poem sound poem
poem sound poem sound sound poem sound poem
poem sound poem soundsoundsoundsound poem sound poem
poem sound poem poem soundsoundsoundsound poem poem sound sound poem
poem sound poem poem sound poem
poem poem sound poem poem sound poem
poem sound poempoempoempoempoempoempoempoempoempoem sound poem
poem sound poempoempoempoempoempoempoempoempoempoem sound poem
sound poem sound poem sound poem sound poem
poem sound sound poem
poem sound sound poem
poem soundsoundsoundsoundsoundsoundsoundsoundsoundsoundsoundsound poem
poem soundsoundsoundsoundsoundsoundsoundsoundsoundsoundsoundsound poem
poem poem
poem poem sound poem sound poem poem
poem poem
poem poem
poempoempoempoempoempoempoempoempoempoempoempoempoempoempoempoempoempoempoempoempoempoem
poempoempoempoempoempoempoempoempoempoempoempoempoempoempoempoempoempoempoempoempoempoem
poem sound poem sound poem
sound poem sound poem sound poem
dsoundsoundsoundsoundsoundsoundsoundsoundsoundsoundsoundsoundsoundsoundsoundsoundsoundsoundsoun
dsoundsoundsoundsoundsoundsoundsoundsoundsoundsoundsoundsoundsoundsoundsoundsoundsoundsoundsoun
poem sound poem sound sound
oempoempoempoempoempoempoempoempoempoempoempoempoempoempoempoempoempoempoempoempoempoempoempoe
oempoempoempoempoempoempoempoempoempoempoempoempoempoempoempoempoempoempoempoempoempoempoempoe
sound poem sound poem sound poem sou

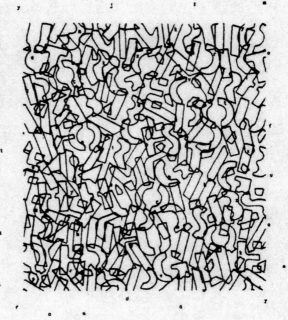

we

we abandon we abbreviate we aberrate we abet we abhor we abide we abolish we abort we abridge we absolve we absorb we abstain we abstract we abuse we accentuate we accept we acclaim we acclimatize we accommodate we accompany we accomplish we accredit we accumulate we accuse we ache we achieve we acknowledge we acquiesce we acquire we acquit we activate we actualize we add we address we adduce we adjourn we adjudicate we adjust we administer we admire we admit we admonish we adopt we adore we adorn we adulate we adulterate we advance we advertise we advise we advocate we affiliate we affirm we affix we age we aggravate we agree we aid we ail we aim we air we alarm we alibi we alienate we allege we allegorize we alleviate we alliterate we allocate we allot we allow we alphabetize we alter we amalgamate we amaze we amend we amuse we anaesthetize we analogize we analyze we anchor we angle we animate we annex we annihilate we annotate we annoy we annul we anoint we answer we antagonize we antedate we anticipate we apologize we apostatize we apostrophize we appall we appeal we appear we appease we applaud we apply we appoint we appraise we appreciate we apprehend we apprentice we approach we appropriate we approve we approximate we arbitrate we argue we arise we arm we arouse we arrange we arrest we arrive we articulate we ascertain we ask we assimilate we assist we associate we assume we assure we astonish we atomize we atone we attach we attack we attain we attempt we attend we attract we attribute we auction we audit we augment we authenticate we authorize we autograph we avenge we average we avert we avoid we avow we await we awake we award we babble we baby we back we badger we baffle we bait we bake we balance we ban we banish we banter we baptize we bar we bare we bargain we barter we bask we baste we bathe we battle we bear we beat we beautify we becalm we become we befriend we beg we beget we begin we behave we behold we belabour we belie we believe we belittle we bellow we belong we bend we benefit we bequeath we bereave we beseech we besiege we bet we betray we better we bevel we beware we bewitch we bewilder we bicycle we bid we bide we bill we bind we bisect we bitch we bite we blabber we blame we bleed we blend we bless we blink we block we blot we blotch we blow we blubber we bluff we blunder we blurt we blush we bluster we board we boast we bond we boss we bother we bottle we bounce we bow we boycott we brag we brand we brawl we break we breathe we breech we breed we brew we bribe we bridge we bring we bristle we broach we broaden we brood we browse we bruise we brush we buckle we build we bully we bump we bunch we bungle we burn we burnish we bury we buy we calculate we call we camouflage we camp we campaign we cancel we capitalize we capitulate we carry we carve we catch we categorize we cause we caution we cavort we cease we cement we censor we centre we certify we chair we challenge we champion we change we channel we charge we charm we chart we chase we chat we cheat we check we cheer we cherish we chew we chide we chill we choke we choose we chop we chronicle we circulate we cite we civilize we claim we clamour we clap we clash we classify we clean we clear we climb we clip we clog we close we clothe we clown we clutter we coast we cohabit we cohere we collaborate we collect we colour we comb we combat we comfort we command we commemorate we commend we comment we commission we commit we communicate we compare we compel we compete we complain we complement we complete we compli-cate we comply we compose we compound we comprehend we compress we comprise we compromise we conceal we concede we conceive we concentrate we conciliate we conclude we concoct we concur we condemn we condescend we condition we condone we conduct we confess we con-fide we confirm we confiscate we conflict we conform we confound we confront we confuse we congratulate we conjecture we connect we connote we conquer we consecrate we consent we conserve we consider we consign we conspire we construct we consult we consume we consummate we contact we contaminate we contain we contemplate we contend we contest we continue we contract we contradict we contrast we contribute we contrive we control we convalesce we converse we convey we convict we convince we cook we co-operate we co-ordinate we cope we copulate we copy we corner we correct we correspond we cough we counsel we count we court we cover we crack we cram we cramp we crank we crash we crave we crawl we create we credit we cringe we criticize we cross we crush we cuddle we cue we cultivate we curry we curse we cushion we cut we cycle we dabble we dally we damage we dance we dare we dash we daunt we deal we debate we debit we debut we decay we deceive we decide we decipher we declare we decode we decorate we decoy we decree we dedicate we deduce we defeat we defect we defend we defer we defy we deify we delay we delegate we delete we deliberate we delight we delineate we deliver we demand we democratize we demolish we demonstrate we demur we denote we deny we depart we depend we depict we deplete we deploy we deport we depose we deposit we deprive we deride we describe we desert we deserve we design we designate we desire we despair we despatch we destroy we detach we detail we detain we detect we deter we determine we detour we develop we devise we devour we diagnose we dictate we die we diet we differ we diffuse we dig we digest we dignify we dilute we diminish we dine we direct we discard we discern we discipline we discriminate we discuss we disguise we dislike we dismantle we dismiss we dispatch we dispel we dispense we disperse we dispose we dispute we dissect we dissent we dissipate we dissociate we distance we distinguish we distort we distract we distribute we disturb we diverge we divert we divide we divorce we divulge we document we dodge we dominate we donate we doze we dramatize we draw we dream we drift we drink we drive we drop we dry we dump we dupe we duplicate we dwell we earn we eat we economize we edify we educate we efface we eject we elaborate we elect we elegize we elevate we elicit we eliminate we elope we elucidate we elude we emancipate we embalm we embarass we embark we embellish we embezzle we embrace we empathize we emphasize we employ we empty we emulate we enchant we enclose we encourage we endanger we endeavor we endorse we endow we endure we enforce we engage we engineer we engrave we enhance we enjoy we enlighten we enroll we enter we entertain we enthrall we entice we entitle we enumerate we envelop we envisage we envy we epitomize we equate we equip we equivocate we eradicate we erode we err we escape we escort we espouse we establish we esteem we estimate we eulogize we evacuate we evade we evict we exacerbate we exaggerate we exalt we examine we exasperate we excavate we excel we excerpt we exchange we exclaim we exclude we excuse we execute we exercise we exhale we exhaust we exhibit we exhort we exist we exit we expand we expatiate we expect we expectorate we expedite we expel we expend we experience we experiment we explain we explete we exploit we expose we expound we express we expropriate we extemporize we extend we externalize we extol we extort we extract we extricate we exult we eye we face we fade we fail we faint we fake we fall we falsify we falter we fancy we fantasize we fascinate we fashion we fast we father we fathom we fatten we favour we fear we feast we feature we feign we fell we fence we fetch we fetter we feud we fictionalize we fidget we fight we figure we file we fill we film we filtrate we finalize we

finance we find we fine we finish we fire we fit we fix we flap we flatten
we flaunt we flavour we flaw we flee we fleece we flex we fling we flip
we flirt we flog we flop we flounder we flourish we flout we focus we foil
we fold we follow we fool we forbid we force we forecast we forego we
foresee we forfeit we forge we forget we forgive we formulate we forsake
we fortify we forward we foster we fracture we fragment we frame we free
we freelance we freeze we frequent we freshen we fret we frighten we frown
we fry we fuel we fulfil we fumble we function we fund we furnish we fuss
we gain we galvanize we gamble we garble we gargle we garner we garnish
we gasp we gather we gauge we gaze we geminate we generalize we generate
we germinate we gesticulate we gesture we get we giggle we gild we gird
we give we glance we glare we glean we glide we glimpse we gloat we
glorify we gloss we glower we glue we glut we gnarl we gnash we go we
gorge we gossip we gouge we govern we grab we grade we graduate we graft
we grant we graph we grapple we grasp we grease we greet we grieve we
grin we grind we grip we groan we groom we groove we grope we grow we
guarantee we guard we guess we guffaw we guide we gulp we gurgle we
haggle we halt we halve we hammer we handle we hang we harass we har-
bour we harmonize we harness we harvest we hasten we hate we haul we
have we heal we hear we heave we heckle we hedge we heed we help we
hew we hiccup we hide we highlight we hint we hire we hiss we hit we
hitch we hoard we hob-nob we hock we hoe we hoist we hold we holiday
we honour we hook we hoot we hop we hope we horrify we host we house
we hover we howl we huddle we hug we hum we humanize we humiliate
we humour we hunger we hunt we hurl we hurry we hurt we hush we
hustle we hyperbolize we hyphenate we hypnotize we hypothesize we
idealize we identify we idolize we ignite we ignore we illicit we illuminate
we illustrate we imagine we imbibe we imitate we immigrate we immolate
we immunize we impair we impart we impeach we impede we impel we
impersonate we impinge we implant we implicate we implore we imply we
impose we impoverish we impregnate we impress we imprison we improve
we improvise we impute we inaugurate we incapacitate we incarcerate we
incite we incline we include we incorporate we increase we incriminate we
incur we indemnify we index we indicate we indict we individualize we
induce we induct we indulge we industrialize we inflate we inflect we inflict
we influence we inform we infringe we inhabit we inhale we inherit we
inhibit we initial we injure we inquire we inscribe we insert we insinuate

we insist we inspire we install we instigate we institute we instruct we insulate we insult we insure we intend we intercede we intercept we interfere we intersect we intervene we interview we intimate we introduce we intrude we inundate we invade we inveigh we invent we invert we invest we investigate we invite we invoke we involve we irrigate we irritate we isolate we itemize we jab we jail we jeer we jest we jet we jilt we jockey we jog we joke we journey we judge we juggle we jumble we jump we justify we juxtapose we keep we kick we kid we kidnap we kill we kindle we kiss we knead we kneel we knit we knock we knot we know we label we labour we lace we lack we lament we lampoon we lance we land we languish we lapse we lash we last we latch we laugh we launch we lay we layer we lead we lean we leap we learn we lease we leave we lecture we legalize we legislate we legitimate we lend we let we level we levy we license we lift we like we limit we limp we linger we link we list we literalize we litigate we litter we live we load we loaf we loan we lobby we localize we locate we lock we lodge we log we long we look we loot we lope we lose we lounge we love we lower we lullaby we lunch we lunge we lurch we lure we lurk we lust we luxuriate we lynch we machinate we magnify we mail we maintain we make we manacle we manage we manipulate we manoeuvre we manufacture we map we march we mark we market we marry we marvel we mash we mask we masquerade we massacre we massage we master we match we mate we matriculate we mature we measure we mechanize we meddle we mediate we meditate we meet we mellow we memorize we menace we mend we mention we merchandize we metabolize we migrate we militarize we mince we mine we mind we mingle we minimalize we minister we mint we miss we mistake we mix we moan we mock we model we moderate we modify we modulate we moisten we molest we mollify we monitor we monopolize we moralize we mortgage we mortify we mother we mould we mount we mourn we move we mow we muffle we multiply we mumble we munch we murder we murmur we muster we mutilate we mutter we muzzle we mystify we mythologize we nag we nail we name we nap we narrate we narrow we nationalize we naturalize we navigate we near we need we needle we negate we negotiate we net we neuter we nibble we nick we nod we nominate we note we notice we notify we nourish we nudge we nullify we number we nurse we nurture we nuzzle we obey we obfuscate we oblige we obliterate we obscure we obstruct we obtain we occupy we offend we offer we omit we open we operate we oppose we oppress we ordain we order we organize we originate we oscillate we ostracize we outline we overcome we overlook we overpower we override we overtake we overturn we overwhelm we owe we own we pace we pacify we pack we pad we paginate we paint we palaver we palliate we palpitate we pamper we pander we panic we paralyse we paraphrase we parcel we pardon we parent we parenthesize we park we parley we parody we parole we part we partake we participate we party we pass we paste we patch we patrol we patronize we pattern we pause we pave we paw we pawn we pay we peck we peculate we peddle we peel we peep we peer we pelt we pen we penalize we pencil we penetrate we pension we perambulate we perceive we perch we perfect we perforate we perform we perish we permeate we permit we perorate we perpend we perpetrate we perpetuate we persecute we persist we personalize we perspire we persuade we perturb we peruse we pervade we pester we pet we petrify we philander we philosophize we photograph we phrase we pick we picket we picnic we picture we pierce we pile we pilfer we pillage we pin we pinch we pine we pioneer we pipe we pirate we pitch we pity we placard we placate we place we plan we plant we plaster we play we plea we please we pledge we plot we plough we plug we plunder we pluralize we ply we poach we pocket we point we poke we polarize we police we polish we poll we pollute we ponder we popularize we populate we portray we pose we position we possess we post we postpone we postulate we posture we pour we pout we practice we praise we pray we prearrange we precede we precipitate we preclude we predicate we predict we pre-empt we preen we preface we prefer we prejudice we prepare we prescribe we present we preserve we preside we press we pressure we presume we pretend we prevail we prevent we prey we price we print we privatize we prize we probe we proceed we process we proclaim we procrastinate we procure we produce we profess we profile we profit we proffer we prognosticate we progress we prohibit we project we prolong we promise we promote we pronounce we propagate we propel we proport we propose we proposition we propound we prorogue we proscribe we prosecute we proselytize we prosper we protect we protest we prove we provide we provoke we prowl we pry we psychoanalize we publish we pull we pulsate we pulverize we pump we pun we punch we punctuate we puncture we punish we purchase we purge we purify we pursue we push we put we puzzle we quaff we qualify we quantify we quarantine we quarrel we quarter we quash we quaver we quell we quench we question we queue we quibble we quicken we quiet we quip we quit we quiver we quiz we quote we race we raffle we raid we raise we rake we rally we ramble we ransack we rap we rape we rate we ratify we rationalize we ravage we raze we reach we read we realize we reap we reason we rebel we rebound we rebuff we rebuke we recant we recede we receive we recess we reciprocate we recite we reckon we recline we recognize we recollect we recommend we reconcile we reconnoitre we record we recruit we rectify we recuperate we redeem we reduce we refer we refine we reflect we reform we refrain we refresh we refund we refurbish we refuse we refute we regain we regard we regenerate we register we regress we regret we regulate we regurgitate we rehabilitate we rehearse we reimburse we reinforce we reinstate we reiterate we reject we rejoice we rejuvenate we relate we relax we release we relegate we relent we relinquish we relish we remain we remark we remedy we remember we reminisce we remit we remove we rendezvous we renew we renounce we renovate we rent we repair we repay we repeal we repeat we repent we replace we reply we report we repress we reprimand we reproach we repudiate we request we require we rescue we resemble we reserve we reside we resign we resist we resolve we respect we respond we rest we restore we restrain we restrict we resume we resuscitate we retain we retaliate we retire we retract we retreat we retrieve we return we reveal we revel we revere we reverse we review we revise we revive we revoke we revolt we reward we ride we rig we rinse we rip we rise we risk we roam we roll we romanticize we row we rub we ruffle we ruin we rule we ruminate we run we rupture we rush we sacrifice we salute we salvage we sample we sanctify we sanction we sanitize we satiate we satirize we satisfy we saturate we saunter we save we savor we scamper we scandalize we scare we schedule we scheme we scoff we scold we score we scorn we scour we scowl we scramble we scrap we scrape we scratch we scrawl we scream we scribble we scrub we scrutinize we scuffle we sculpture we scuttle we seal we search we season we secrete we section we secularize we secure we sedate we seduce we see we seed we seek we segment we segregate we seize we select we sell we send we sense we sentence we sentimentalize we separate we sequester we serenade we sermonize we serve we settle we sever we sew we shade we shake we shame we shape we share we shatter we shelve we shingle we shirk we shiver we shock we shoot we shop we shorten we shout we shove we show we shower we shriek we shrug we shudder we shuffle we shun we shut we sigh we sign we signal we silence we simplify we sin we sing we singe we sip we sire we sit we skate we skedaddle we skewer we ski we skid we skin we skip we skirt we slacken we slam we slander we slant we slap we slash we slay we sleep we slice we slide we slip we slit we slouch we slur we smash we smear we smile we smooth we smother we smuggle we snack we snap we snare we snatch we sneak we sneer we sneeze we sniff we snip we snivel we snore we snort we snub we snuggle we soak we sob we socialize we solicit we soliloquize we solve we sour we span we spank we spare we speak we specialize we specify we speculate we spell we spend we spice we spill we spin we spit we spite we splash we split we spoil we sponsor we spot we sprain we sprawl we spray we spread we spring we sprinkle we sprint we spurn we spy we squabble we squander we squash we squat we squawk we squeeze we squirm we stabilize we stack we staff we stage we stagger we stagnate we stain we stalk we stall we stamp we stand we standardize we stare we starve we stay we steady we steal we steer we step we stereotype we sterilize we stifle we stigmatize we stimulate we stipulate we stitch we stock we stop we store we straddle we straighten we strain we strangle we strap we stray we stretch we stride we strike we strip we strive we stroke we stroll we structure we struggle we study we stuff we stumble we stylize we subdue we subject we subjugate we sublimate we submerge we submit we subordinate we subpoena we subscribe we subsidize we sub- stitute we subtitle we subtract we subvert we succeed we succumb we sue we suffer we suffocate we suffuse we suggest we summarize we summon we sup we superimpose we superintend we supersede we supervise we supplement we supply we support we suppose we suppress we surmise we surprise we surrender we surround we survey we survive we suspect we suspend we sustain we swagger we swallow we swear we sweat we sweep we swim we swindle we swing we syllogize we symbolize we symmetrize we sympathize we synthesize we systematize we table we tackle we tailor we taint we take we talk we tally we tame we tamper we tan we tangle we tango we tantalize we tap we tape we tar we target we tarnish we tarry we taste we tattoo we taunt we tax we teach we tease we tell we tempt we test we tether we thank we thematize we theologize we theorize we theosophize we think we thirst we threaten we thrive we throng we throw we thrust we thwart we tickle we tidy we tie we tighten we till we tilt we time we tinker we tint we tip we tire we title we toast we toil we tolerate we topple we torture we toss we touch we tour we tow we trace we track we trade we trail we train we transact we transcend we transcribe we transfer we transfigure we transform we transgress we translate we transliterate we transmit we transplant we transport we transpose we trap we travel we treasure we tremble we trespass we trick we trim we triumph we trivialize we trot we trudge we try we tug we tumble we tune we tunnel we turn we tutor we twist we twitch we type we underestimate we understand we understate we undertake we undress we unify we unionize we unite we universalize we unleash we unmask we untie we uphold we uproot we upset we urge we use we usher we usurp we utilize we utter we vacate we vaccinate we vacillate we value we vanquish we varnish we vaunt we veer we venerate we vent we venture we verbalize we verify we versify we veto we vex we victimize we view we vilify we vindicate we violate we visualize we vitalize we vivify we vivisect we vocalize we vociferate we volunteer we vomit we vote we vouch we vow we voyage we wade we wage we wait we wake we walk we wall we wallop we wallow we waltz we wander we wangle we war we warn we warrant we wash we waste we watch we water we waver we wear we weave we weed we weep we weigh we welcome we wheedle we whimper we whine we whip we whisper we whistle we whither we whittle we widen we wield we will we wink we wipe we wire we wish we withdraw we wither we withhold we withstand we witness we wonder we work we worry we worship we wound we wrap we wreck we wriggle we wrinkle we write we xerox we x-ray we yawn we yearn we yield we yodel we zig-zag we zip we zipper we zone we surveys

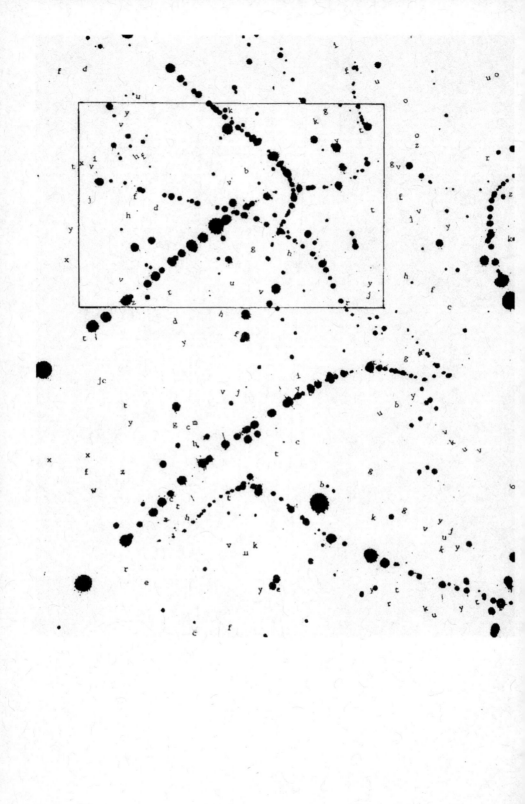

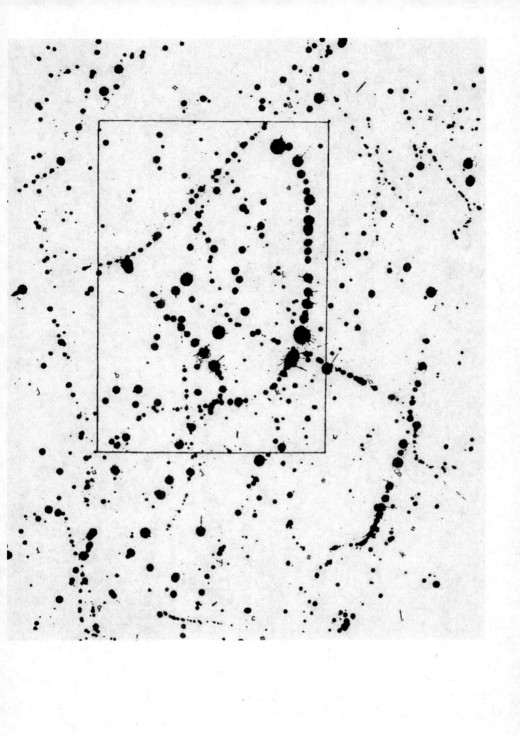

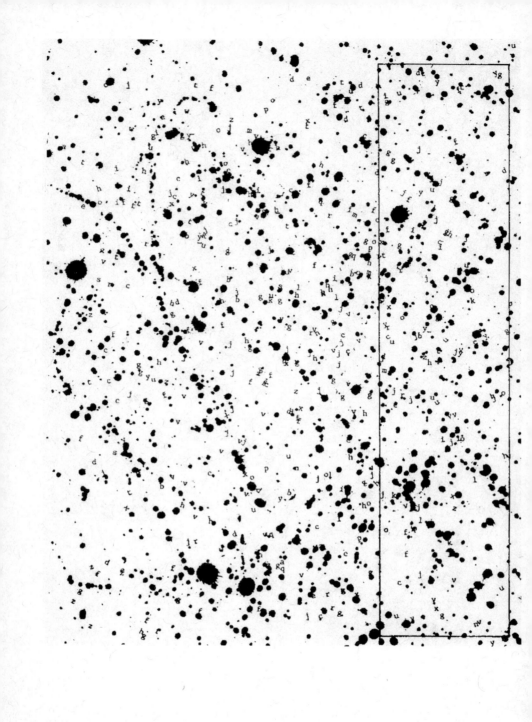

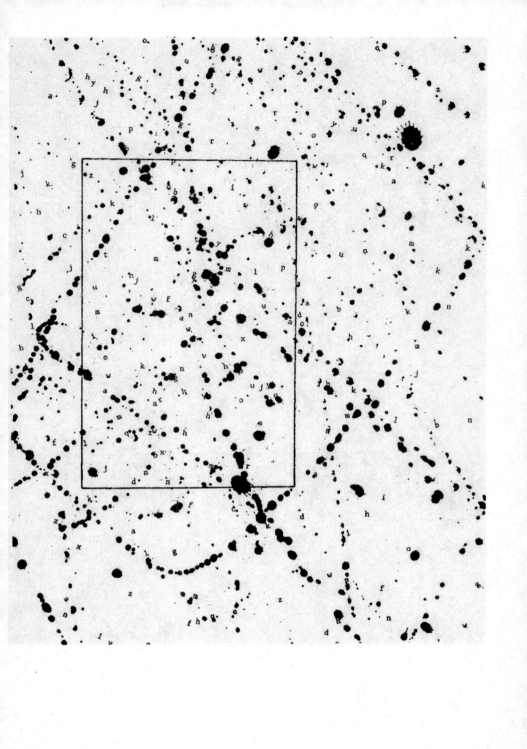

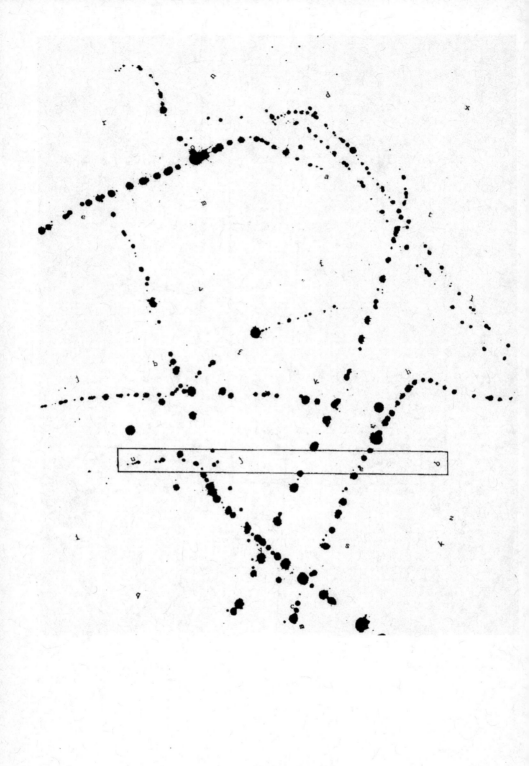

runes

a shredded text

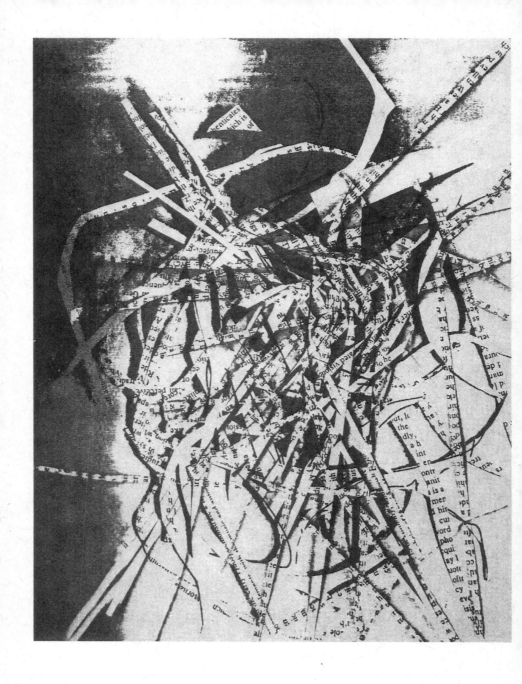

in take

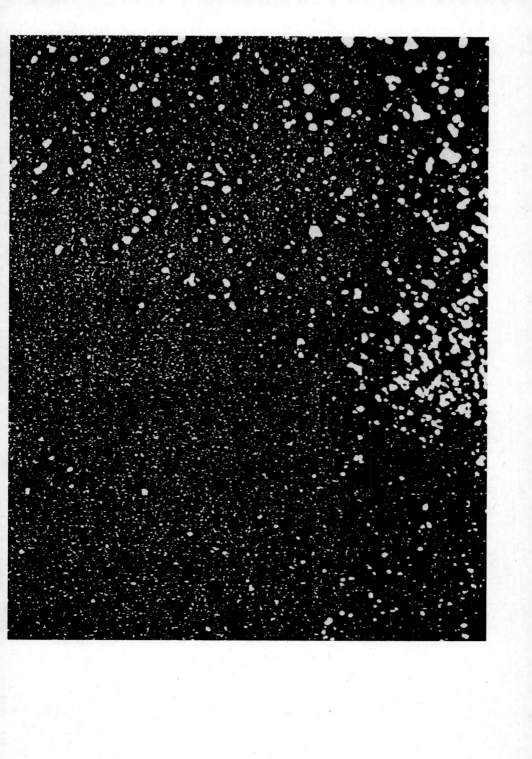

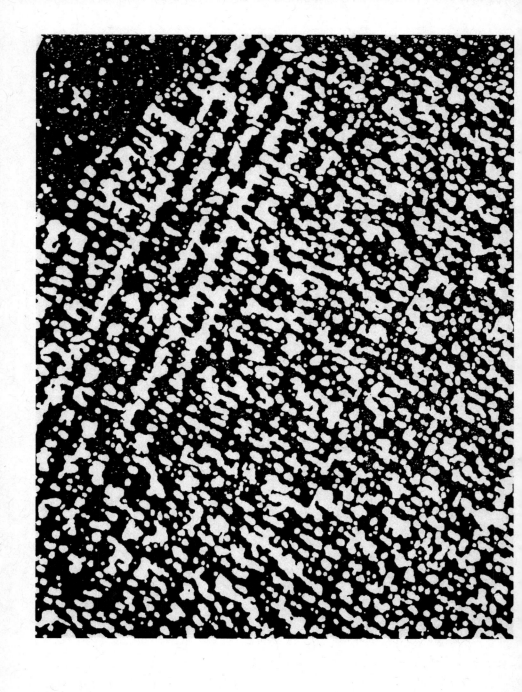

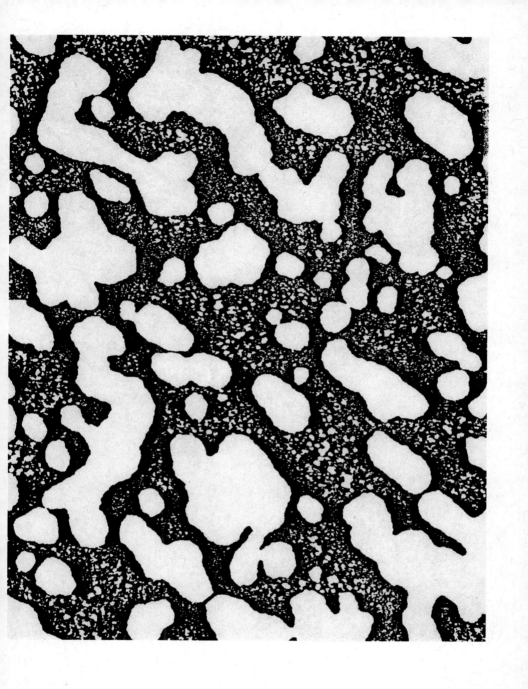

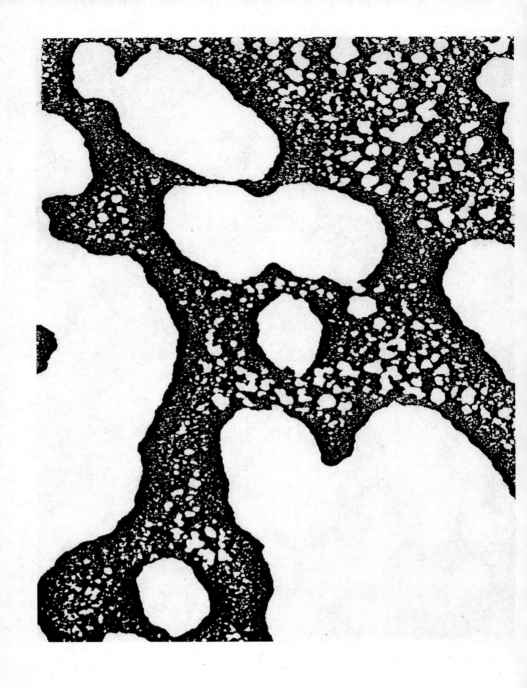

watching

a to o

nal f

o a g

ted to

lonal f

to a g

televis

lotted to

nctional f

ned to a g

ch televis

oices inhe

inal versi

e alotted to
functional f
nfined to a s
watch televis
choices inhe
a final versi
ee in greater
them that th
t h   l ft i

ne role alotted to
in the functional f
be confined to a s
or to watch televis
other choices inhe
se of a final versi
n to see in greater
on to them that th
ones to be left in
cking of the hall o
ue which she refuse
to discuss such mat

coda

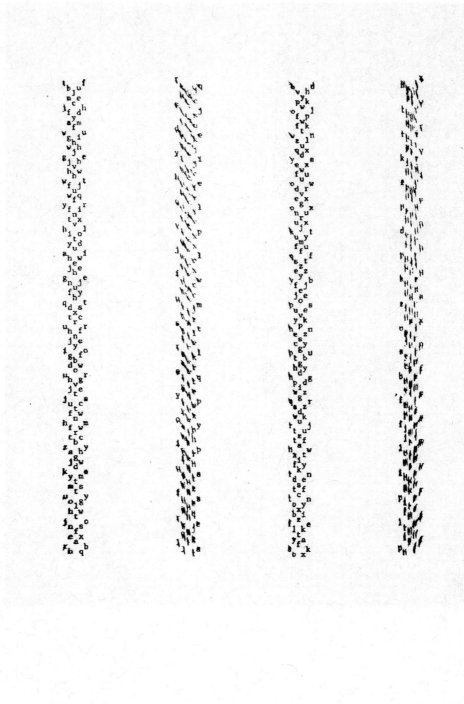

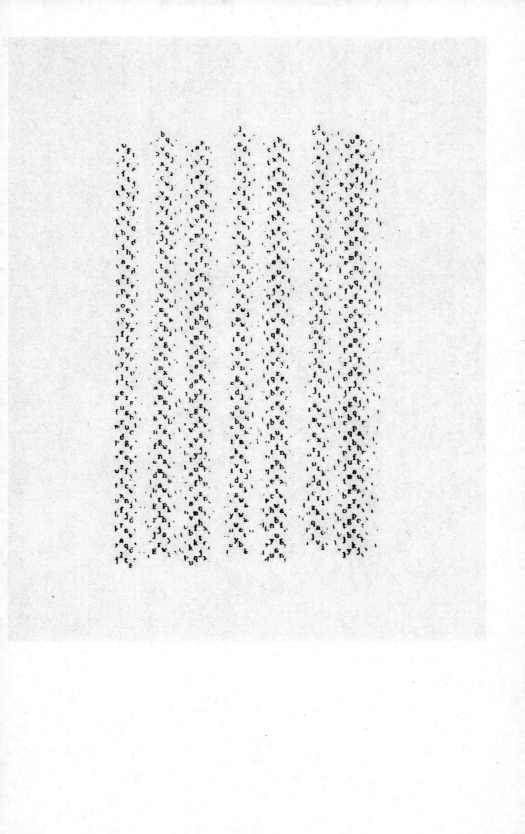

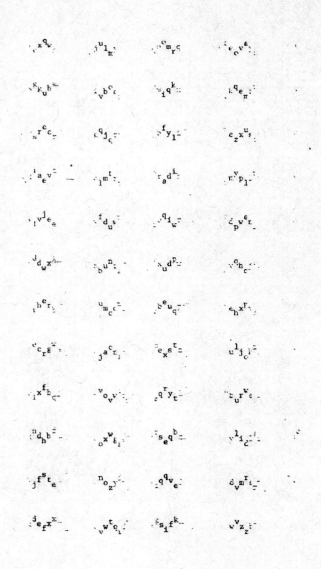

untitled

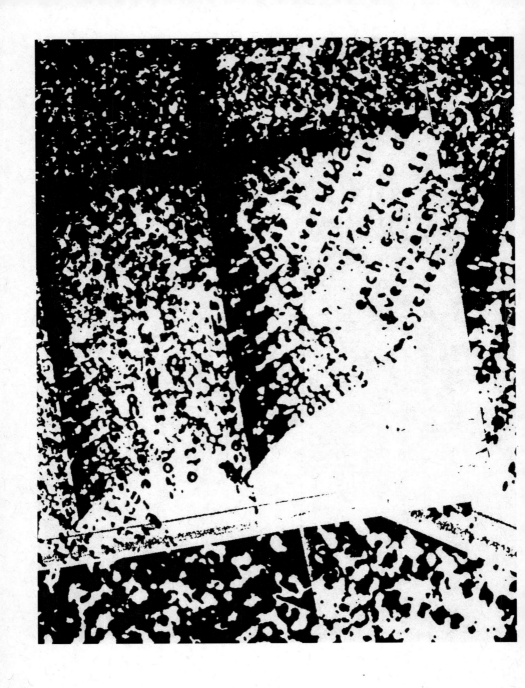

Traces

ness by adherence to a single detail of repeating sig-
nifiers which left many of us cold although i had al-
ready closed the window & opened the fridge for some
food for all that walking had made me hungry made my-
self a sandwich i listened to the sound of my own si-
lence encapsulated within such a small space of living
don't you think i often attempt to turn my attention
to those very concerns which may well have been quite
other than what one might have expected nevertheless i
could not in all honesty refrain from further explora-
tion of the effects of these & like devices (i call
them 'tactical') (however all this to be taken from
no small amount of concern for the subject) all the
while (being as yet unable to reach others with little
more than a few words on the matter) -wherein it seems
to me many of us have all lost a great deal in the pr-
ocess of coming back to the idea of research circa the
smallest of particles/particulars in order to release/
uncover those very embellishments we had earlier on
(so often) tended to dismiss as either 'meaningless,'
or 'meaningful' (currently understood to connect with
those very trace structures it so often appears we had
(in an historical sense) started out with) even now
before i undress lay down & sleep in spite of the cha-
nces so many of us take in order to achieve some small
gain in some equally small project undertaken in an

waters which filled my mind with a variety of abstract
images & sat & stared for a moment into the black dis-
tance   (it was overcast by then)   in contrast to   the
bright lights behind me falling on the edge of two so
called 'realities' the natural & the manmade extended
& improved upon without too much concern for   the
'other' as then presented in an inkblack face facing
south & hoped for the best walked back along a quiet
sidestreet (having decided the main thoroughfares were
too crowded too noisy too distracting for my contem-
plative frame of mind) passed by the very coffee shop
i had sat in earlier on (nipped in for a quiet cup) by
now along familiar sidestreets towards the place where
i live appears to be more in my head than elsewhere
depending upon friends interests & events as they move
in & out of relation to one another along this thin
fragile line of thought i thought i had answered long
ago (but was mistaken) climbed the stairs opened the
door turned the lights on looked briefly out the wi-
ndow took my jacket off stared at my reflection for a
moment in the bathroom mirror my mind a blank piece of
literature lying on the floor i had thought i had left
on the reading table' the wind must have blown it off'
i thought (my back window had been thoughtlessly le-
ft open) picked it up & began to read an outline of
one writer's desire to raise our level of conscious-

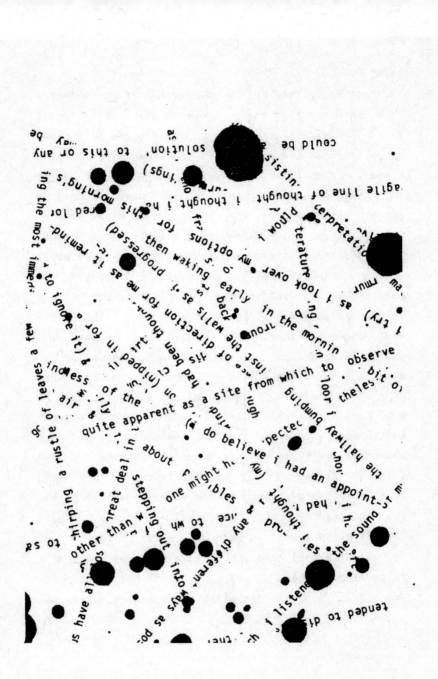

could be s... sistin' solution to this or any way be

agile line of thought i thought i would ... cerpretatio

ing the most imm... red for ... for this morning's hu... pillow i terature as i look over my options for ... my options

then waking early in the morning

to remind ... as it... back ... progressed

to ignore it) & ...e of direction for me as i... the walls as i progressed

had been thou... art (nipped in for a

quite apparent as a site from which to observe the hallway bumping theles

air ...indless of the

or a rustle of leaves a few

about one might h... do believe i had an appoint-

chirping stepping out into ... other than ... great deal in ... ibles to wh... any differen...

i... listen... the sound tended to di...

is have al...

movement & shift from one style to another geographic-
ally or topologically integrating the ebb & flow of a
time structured to include us at the moment of this
writing as is those frames stare back at us through
the myopic lens of current research on our respective
philosophical projects as enlarged to me one day as I
was simply strolling down a street wondering about
some of the issues of the day I had just read about in
the newspaper in a coffee shop I had just left not
going anywhere in particular just thought I would go
for a walk (it seemed such a pleasant afternoon) to
clear the air & think about possibles & probables
which are in fact those very items (re)arranged on a
plate of food I had munched on in the coffee shop won-
dering about those who glanced in at me through the
windows as they passed by the sun fell on the pen I
used to write down some of the evidence which has re-
mained much as I have (or will have) presented it to
you in the hope that you will understand my predica-
ment insofar as I make it clear to you the way I per-
ceive these things (my surroundings) as they may be
glass coffee paper friends the occasional cigarette
which had been lit by a man who sat across the restau-
rant from where I was before my feet shuffled through

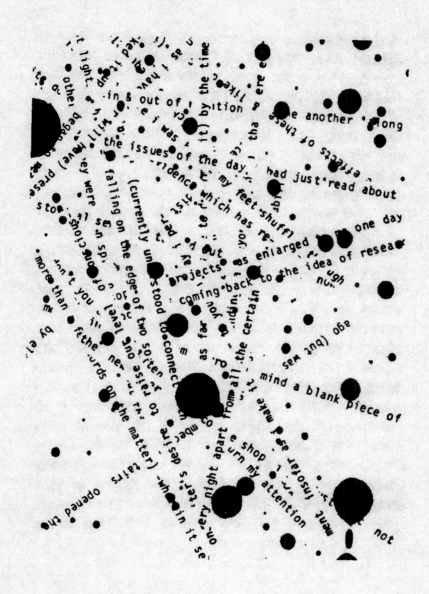

me hungry

though   spuewards   -be me hungry

exper   too distractin   glass

there are many alternatives   to th

too crowded   from one style to another geographic-

traces   of an effort   is required

time   to include us   at the

subject/o

relations

one) i m myopic lens of curr   leave off now   so often b

ness   adherence to a sing   detail of rep

rrible!) effects such an attitu   prose ex   with the in

a large collection of leaves (autumn) suddenly realiz-
ing the most immediate book I had leafed through re-
ally had no relevance to what I was trying to say al-
though each page contained at least a few words which
signalled some sense of direction for me as it remind-
ed me that I once used to call names as they arose as
other than they were (in spite of the fact that this
might all seem as so much gibberish to you (I can cer-
tainly sympathize with your reaction) although I also
was hoping you might be able to appreciate my dilemma
as far as I am able to determine it) by the time I re-
ached the end of the street I turned down some other
mindless of the time (I do believe I had an appoint-
ment elsewhere that day which I subsequently missed)
assuming not too much of an effort is required to re-
cognize the spacial elements of a derivative prose ex-
tending far beyond any idea that there ever would or
could be a 'final solution' to this or any other set
of problematics insofar as we have witnessed the de-
bilitating (if not horrible) effects such an attitude
can result in finally getting home later on that night
after having walked all the way down to the harbour
front sat by the water's edge listening to the acous-
tic 'ping' of the water splash off the sides of nearby
buildings the traffic a discrete (somewhat soothing)
murmur in the background as distinct from the inklike

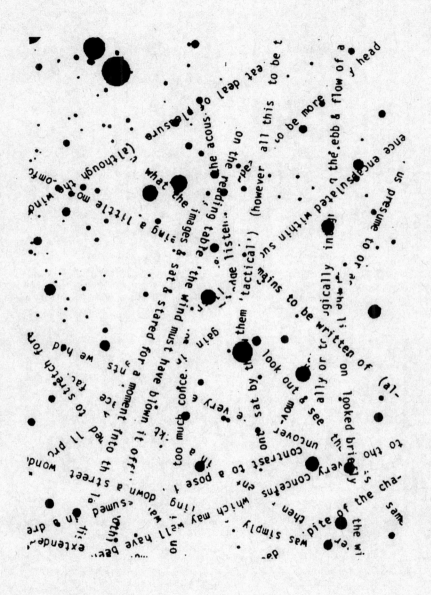

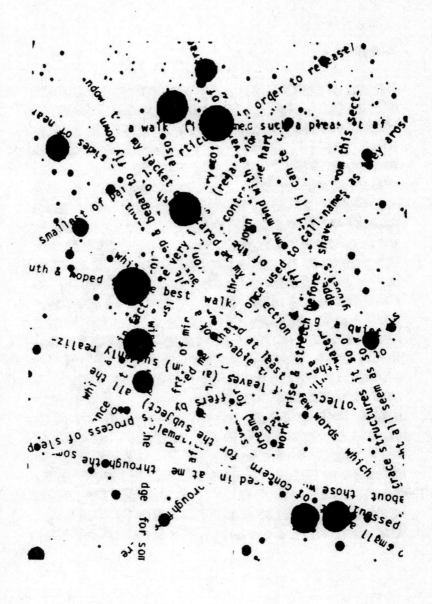

attempt to distance oneself from pain by eliminating
subject/object relations as has so often been done by
now wondering if the affinity the two have for each
other either gains or suffers by this process of sleep-
ing together which arouses me with the idea of turning
over on one side as being a little more comfortable in
contrast to a pose I had assumed in a dream I had that
very night apart from all the certainties & capabili-
ties each of us presume to or actually do possess mov-
ing around a small room touching each spot on each wall
in as many different ways as possible gave to me a
great deal of pleasure (although the window itself was
quite apparent as a site from which to observe I ten-
ded to ignore it) & finally left by stepping out into
the hallway which seemed to stretch forward (in the
dream) forever I took a single step & began to fly down
the hallway bumping against the walls as I progressed)
then waking early in the morning a bit of light some
sparrows chirping a rustle of leaves a few more fall-
ing when I look out & see the (this) same familiar
location (resisting interpretation no matter how hard
I try) as I look over my options for this morning's
work rise & stretch before I shave off from this sect-
ion what there is still remains to be written of (al-
though I expect there are many alternatives to this
one) I must leave off now to tend to matters elsewhere

from Glass

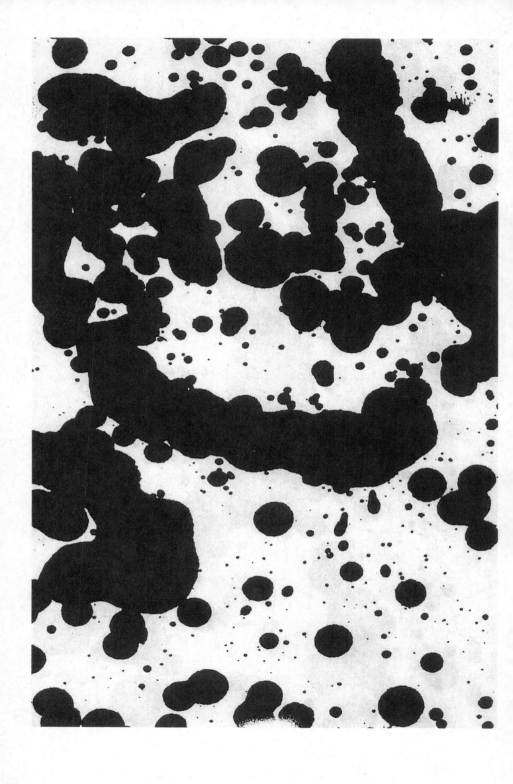

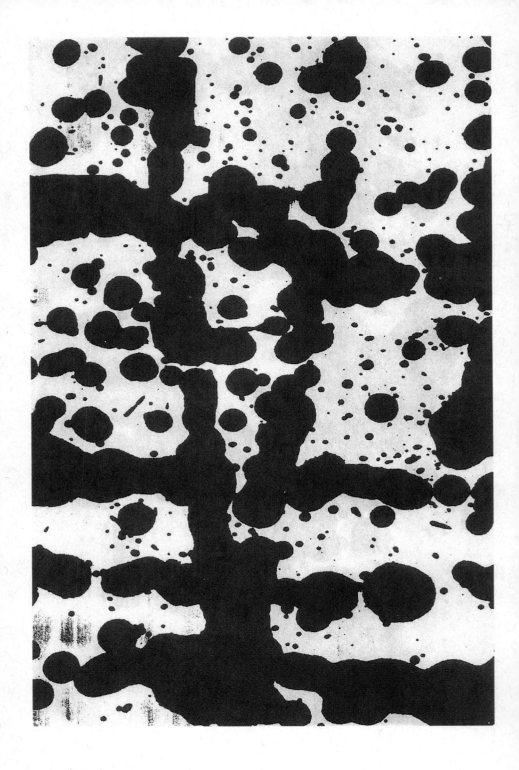

In the ... which followed ... of clarity ... of ... inserted a mismatched ... which is ... during which the ...

... that is being ... that there ... densita ... the fit ... her)

... should ...

... be a more or less ...

... pattern in ... the amount of ... material itself ... of us should the ...

... telling about ... always intere... a bit ... exciting ... to the base ...

... of the scored material (much of it on page 9) empl... ... within the structure of the ... of the ... ... those of us who ... the ...

... the category ... ... clarity and form which ... had grown

Selected Works of John Riddell

Pope Leo, El ELoPE: A Tragedy in Four Letters. Toronto: Ganglia Press, 1969.

"untitled." *grOnk* 3:8 (1970).

A Hole in the Head. Toronto: grOnk, [1975].

Priapus Arched and *Morox*. With Richard Truhlar. *Kontakte* 1.1. Toronto: Phenomenon Press, [1976].

Criss-cross: a Text Book of Modern Composition. Toronto: Coach House Press, 1977.

Mark Lalonde. Toronto: Presspol, n.d.

Transitions. Toronto: Aya Press, 1980.

War [Words at Roar], Vol. 1: s/word/s games. Toronto: Underwhich Editions, 1981.

War, Vol. 2 – Words at Roar. Toronto: Underwhich Editions, 1983.

Peacing It TOGETHER? Toronto: TBC Productions / Therafields Foundation, [1985].

A Game of Cards. Toronto: Underwhich Editions, 1985.

A Game of Cards, Vol. 2. Toronto: Underwhich Editions, 1986.

"spring." Toronto: Spider Plots in Rat Holes, 1986.

d'Art Board. Toronto: Underwhich Editions, 1986.

d'Art Board. Toronto: privately published, n.d.

a/z does it. London, ON: Nightwood Editions, 1988.

E clips E. Toronto: Underwhich Editions, 1989.

TRACES. Toronto: Gesture Press, 1989, 1991.

Shit. Toronto: letters, 1990.

An Introduction to Social Therapy. Toronto: The Centre, [1994].

The Great Canadian T-Shirt System. Toronto: privately published, [1994].

Lingo! Toronto: CHEX, [1994].

A Game of Cards. Toronto: privately published, 1994.
Glass. Toronto: CHEX, n.d.
The Light Bulb Conspiracy. Toronto: CHEX, n.d.
The Bottle. Toronto: CHEX, n.d.
How to Grow Your Own Light Bulbs. Toronto: privately published, [1995].
How to Grow Your Own Light Bulbs. Stratford, ON: Mercury Press, 1996.
Smokes: a novel mystery. Toronto: Curvd H&z, 1996.

Acknowledgements

Lori Emerson and derek beaulieu would like to thank the following people for their support during the creation of *Writing Surfaces*: Nelson Ball, Christian Bök, jwcurry, Kit Dobson, Paul Dutton, Charlie Huisken, Marvin Sackner, Steven Ross Smith, Richard Truhlar, Darren Wershler, and Eric Zboya. Our poetic communities and online conversations have inspired and excited us into action. Thank you also to Ellie Nichol and the estate of bpNichol for permission to include bpNichol's illustrations in this volume.

Great appreciation to John Riddell for allowing us the opportunity to cast his work into the context of twenty-first-century poetic conversations.

Brian Henderson and Wilfrid Laurier University Press have been excellent to work with and have provided editorial acumen, deadline reinforcement, and all the best kind of support. Thank you.

Grateful acknowledgement to the editors of Aya Press, CHEX, Coach House Press, Ganglia, Gesture Press, *grOnk*, Nightwood Editons, and Underwhich Editions for the original publication of the work in *Writing Surfaces*.

Thank you also to Kristen Beaulieu for patience and breakfast and Ben Robertson for patience and dinner.